"It was then that I found it. Dumped near the path."

"What? Dumped?"

"Like some do with dogs they don't want. Somebody must have pushed it up the track, the other side of the cliff, and it was parked under a hazel. By the side of one of the holes. Drop down there, and it'd be minutes before you hit anything. And when you did . . . I couldn't leave it, could I, the carriage thing? I had to bring it here."

"A carriage? What's the use of that?"

"It's what's inside it." For a moment his tone held a hint of apology. Ren waited. "A baby."

FOUND

JUNE OLDHAM

The Putnam & Grosset Group

A PaperStar Book,
published in 1998 by The Putnam & Grosset Group,
200 Madison Avenue, New York, NY 10016. PaperStar is a
registered trademark of The Putnam Berkley Group, Inc.
The PaperStar logo is a trademark of The Putnam Berkley
Group, Inc. First American edition published in 1996 by Orchard Books.
This novel was first published in a substantially different form
under the title Foundling in 1995 by Hodder Children's Books, England.
Printed in the United States of America
The text of this book is set in Weiss.

Library of Congress Cataloging-in-Publication Data
Oldham, June. [Foundling]
Found / June Oldham.—1st. American ed. p. cm.
"A Melanie Kroupa book"—Half t.p.
Summary: Because her mother cannot afford to keep her, Ren
tries to survive along with other homeless persons who are
united in their determination to care for an abandoned baby.
[1. Abandoned children—Fiction. 2. Homeless persons—Fiction.
3. Survival—Fiction. 4. Babies—Fiction.] I. Title.
PZ7.04539Fo 1996 [Fic]—dc20 96-12992
ISBN 0-698-11674-7

1 3 5 7 9 10 8 6 4 2

For Vida Finney

The time is the twenty-first century
when the countryside is almost deserted,
when people work at computers in living-work units,
and those without work live on the streets,
when in the living-work units there is a tax on excess children,
and when the street people are hounded
by patrols.

Then some seek other places, passing through
the wide valleys
and over the high hills.

And one late autumn, two fleeing from the towns
—and fearing pursuit—
make an unexpected discovery.
They are joined by two other travelers,
and the four remain together
through new perils and threats.

This is their story.
It begins with the smallest of them. Called Ren.

ONE

Ren stood in a crescent formed by tall walls of rock. She was alone now and must fend for herself. High above her, slender trees wagged at the sky. Below her, on the path, she could see the woman who had brought her. She was striding fast over the stones and pebbles, and Ren wished she could make her own legs work, make them run after the woman and make her throat shout: I don't want to be left by myself. Please stay with me. But all that came was a whisper, not enough to startle a bird or cause a nibbling sheep to raise its head. The woman reached the road and climbed into the parked truck. She did not look up the steep slope to Ren's hiding place and wave. Nor did she turn her head to the opposite side of the valley and examine the mountain's long stretch, checking for patrolmen. Ren heard the engine start up; then, in a spray of grit and pebbles, the truck rattled away. It vanished in seconds, and the valley was silent. The truck did not disturb the rocks and boulders that grew out of the grass and browning heathers; it left no echo among the strange cliffs that rose up, striped white and shelved with loose scree.

Ren shuddered. She had never seen anything like this. At home, she rarely left the living-work unit where she lived. "Used to live," she murmured to herself.

"I don't want you to go," her mother had said, "but I can't keep you both and I have to choose the new baby, don't I? You'll be happy with Greta. Things aren't as strict there as they are in this province. Not everyone works at computers all day, and Greta lives in a proper house."

Imagining her mother's distress when she heard what had happened, Ren felt the tears run down her cheeks.

Madge, the woman who brought her, had apologized: "I'm sorry there's been this hitch. It's tough, but I can't hang around. I have to deliver my freight on time or I'll be fired. I'll report that Greta's been held up and someone will come and get you, take you to Greta's place. Or I might even pick you up myself on my way back. Meanwhile, you'll have to wait here. No one will find you, provided you keep out of sight. Remember, you're an absconder now. Don't look so worried. You're not the first. All you have to do is stay hidden; then you'll be safe."

Safe! Safe from patrolmen, the woman had meant. But it was not only their threat that had stopped Ren's breath. There was also the darkness. Had Madge thought of that? Had she ever seen the dusk inch toward her, nearer and nearer every minute, closing the spaces between the trees and bringing the night in its wake? Had Madge ever stood knowing that behind her the ground humped abruptly and disappeared under a rock? Making a deep gash. A waiting hole.

Madge had told her, "It's not a very big cave. Come on! Look!" Frightened, Ren had wanted to remain where she stood; where, dropping through the high leaves, the spots of sun danced. But, obedient, she slithered under the low arch of rock. Immediately blackness wrapped round her; it had no texture or shine. She heard Madge saying, "There is food, bedding. That noise you hear is from a water spout in another chamber, but this one is dry now." Her flashlight showed a litter of pebbles, stones, a stretch of thin mud. Climbing up the walls, the beam picked out strange shapes worn by the drip and polish of water. To Ren they looked like ugly faces and evil masks.

Now the light was gone from the sky. Ren was tired and cold. Her sleeping bag was in the cave behind her. Slowly she forced her feet to step to its entrance. "You see, nothing to be afraid of," Madge had assured her.

But, on the fringe of the flashlight's pale ribbon, the darkness waited, ready and thick.

She could feel it creeping toward her. Ready to spring. Groping for her bag, she told herself she could unroll it, but that she must not lie down. Though she could see nothing either beyond the entrance or in the deep chamber at her back, she must not close her eyes. She must stay awake. When it grew light again, when the day started, the darkness would slide away and it would be safe to sleep. But the night was spinning; she could no longer sit up and her knees were scraping over the stones and she could not prevent her neck from bending to the pillow. Then she felt it cold against her cheek.

Lying on her side, her hands clamped over her head, Ren

saw again the faces that hung on the high chamber's walls. They leered down at her, seemed to swing closer; they fixed their wet lips over her knuckles and sucked. Wrestling them off, she shrieked for help. But no one came. The night sounds swelled around her; the splash of water in the distant chamber grew into a thunderous spate. Shaking, her clothes soaked with sweat, she felt the breath of the cave blow on her neck and crawl up her twitching throat.

Then the darkness swooped upon her, smothered her, and only in the cracks between nightmares did Ren see that the blackness had thinned and had become a tissue of gray. When her brittle sleep was shattered by the crackling of leaves under boots, Ren screamed and tore out of her bag. Dazed, her brain slow with exhaustion, she scrambled from the figure that stood under the cave's arch.

"I wish you'd lay off that whining," a voice said. "I'm only here because I could do with a snack."

The speaker turned to the cans of food, and Ren saw a boy. He was taller than she was, but thinner. "It's soup I'm after. You've not eaten it all?" he asked anxiously.

In answer she stammered, "Has Madge sent you?"

"Never heard of a Madge."

"Then how did you know I was here?"

"Saw."

Ren thought: Since he saw me, perhaps others did, too. Do the officials know where I'm hiding? Will I soon be brought in? Her heart thumped.

Gripping a can, the boy drove a line of perforations around the lid. "Saw the rest of them, too. Been a good few come here."

"What happened to them?"

"You're a jumpy one! Look, my insides are rattling like an

empty drum," he excused his limited sympathy. "It was only me that spotted them. Most cleared out fast. Doubtless they were eager to get moving. I'd not be surprised if they didn't care for this place." He glanced at the darkness behind him, and Ren saw a spasm run down his arm and jerk the fingers encircling the can. It told her that he, too, felt the cave's menace.

She slid closer to him. "I don't like it, either. I've never slept in a place like this before. I lived in a living-work unit, with my mother, only she's expecting a baby."

"What's that got to do with it?"

She was astonished by his ignorance. "Don't you know?"

"Why should I?" he said defensively. "I haven't seen a baby since . . . since I caught sight of one at the back of a truck. Years ago."

"We're not supposed to have more than one 'young person' in the living-work unit."

"That's mad!"

"If there is more than one, we have to pay a tax. My mother couldn't pay it, so I had to be sent away."

"Sounds like you're better off out of that place," he remarked, but Ren shook her head. "Where are you heading now?"

"I don't know. I have to wait to be picked up, Madge said."

"You're not forced to. You can do what you like."

This suggestion surprised her. She asked, "Do you do what you like?" He nodded but offered no explanation. "Don't you have to make sure that the patrolmen can't see you?"

"Of course not! I'm not an absconder like you." He saw her face tremble and added quickly, "Except sometimes, if there's a chore coming up that I don't much care for, I'll do a bit of disappearing myself, double quick."

"Where do you live?"

"In this valley, and the next, and the next." His arm made a gesture, wide and grand. "And I just bed down where it suits me. There're plenty of farmhouses empty, and sheds and barns. Anyplace out of the wind."

That is what the street people do at home, Ren thought. But he was not one of them. He wasn't enormous with tattoos rippled by muscles, his face ferocious and his mouth full of chipped teeth like the street people that were shown on the news-screen. He wasn't loaded down with weapons. All he had was a penknife, and its blade was broken.

"Where did you sleep last night?"

He waved a hand. "Up there in the gully. The ferns are dry."

She had had a guardian! Throughout the long night, someone had been near her. If she had known that, would she have been able to sleep? She heard herself ask, "Will you stay here tonight?"

The boy did not answer her question. He gabbled, "I'm making for a service station, fetching a few supplies. You might say pinching. Only it's a considerable hike and I couldn't last. Looks like I haven't a choice." He held up the can; its lid was puckered and slashed.

"There's an opener. It's not like the one we had at home, but I suppose you could make it work."

He nodded and waited.

She did not move to get it. "I couldn't sleep. Greta should have met me, but she was held up. That's why I'm left here. I've got to wait. In this cave. And I've never . . . there's so much dark . . ."

The boy interrupted. "This soup's on the thick side, but I can suck it out."

"You wouldn't have to if you had an opener. And there are bound to be cans of other things. You can have any you like, if you stay." Her face was red with shame; her voice was shrill with the begging, but she was desperate not to spend another night alone in the cave.

"Stop it!" he ordered, loud. "I'm not listening! You wouldn't ask if you'd heard Mrs. Gimmer. She walked the drovers' ways. She has tales to tell."

"I don't want to hear them."

"Nor me, either. They're daft. They couldn't ever have happened. I say to her, to Mrs. Gimmer, 'What's so special about these Norsemen you go on about? I've never as much as laid eyes on one.' She says to me, 'They didn't belong here at the start; they came in ships, tramped about for a while, then settled down and built farms.' But it seems one of them didn't. He took a fancy to this cave. But that's centuries ago, isn't it? What's it matter to me if he was a giant-sized cannibal?"

Ren put up her hands, muffing her ears.

"You've got nothing to worry about. It wasn't young girls that giant Yordas enjoyed the taste of. It was boys." He had risen. "I'm off now."

She was frantic. She had to grip her hands together; otherwise she would have scrambled over to him and tried to hold him there with her arms looped round his legs. "What's the difference between out there in the dark and in here?"

"There's a difference. If you don't know it, I can't tell you."

"You said it was silly. You said the story could never have happened. If you don't believe it, why are you scared?" She knew that she should not have said that. It wasn't fair to accuse someone of a weakness when you possessed it yourself. Remorseful, she watched his face blanch.

"I'm not scared." Taking a breath, he repeated more loudly, "I'm not scared. I've had more to face in my time than some stupid stories. I'm not scared of bedding down in this cave. So if I'm hereabouts this evening, I'll have a look in."

Ren could tell that the boy didn't want to talk any more about it, so to thank him she rummaged in the box Madge had pointed out and found the strange pincerlike gadget for opening cans.

As the boy ate the soup, using a metal spoon that he took from a pocket, she asked him, "What's your name?"

"Brocket. What's yours?"

"Ren."

"That's nice. Do they often put that name on a girl?"

"I don't know. My mother gave it to me after watching a very old program on the leisure-screen. It was about birds. Mother liked them all, but there was one she liked most. The man on the screen, a horny thologist or something, said it was a ren, so Mother called me that. She said rens are small and shy."

"She's right, and there's nothing wrong with that, is there? Wrens aren't showy and they stay hid. Not easy to catch."

And tinkling the spoon against the empty can, he gave her a large grin.

TWO

Ren laid aside the can of beans she was eating and polished her spoon on the grass. Unheated, the beans had no flavor. Among the supplies in the cave was a contraption that she supposed was designed for cooking; it had a small cannister under it and a support for a pan. But she dared not experiment with it, although she longed for a warm meal. She had never eaten cold beans or cold soup or cold stew. Not even in summer. "And it'll be winter soon," she told herself. Already leaves, yellow and bright tawny, were twisting and skittering down.

She must wear her thicker sweater and the warmer pants. Generally it was only in emergencies that they were used; for example, when the heating in the living-work units did not function. However, her mother had said, "I'm packing these, Ren, because you'll need them at Greta's; you won't spend all day indoors."

"I'd rather stay here. I want to see the baby."

"You will one day, my dear; and we'll exchange messages. We must be thankful that Greta can take you. There's no tax on excess children where she lives. I just want you to be a good girl. Otherwise Greta will think I haven't brought you up properly." Her mother had tried to smile. "And don't catch cold."

So, tomorrow she would put on the thicker sweater and warmer pants. That is, if no one came to get her. She had no idea when anyone might come. Dejected, Ren scraped her boots through twigs, brown, scaled cones, and the droppings of rabbits. Among them were pebbles. She stared at them, then picked up two. "This one is for today," she said to herself, "and this is for yesterday, the day I came." She would add a pebble every morning, to keep a tally of the waiting days.

She had no way to tell the time, having no watch. Watches were unnecessary at home, where the hours, minutes, and seconds always pulsed at a corner of the screens. She did not know whether it was late morning or afternoon, or whether the gray in the sky meant the approach of evening or a storm.

"I suppose it's too late for Madge or Greta or anyone to pick me up today," she muttered, "and the boy didn't promise to come." All the same, she would have a look to see if anyone was coming. She must not let herself think about another night in the cave.

Remembering Madge's order, "You must stay out of sight," Ren stepped cautiously to the edge of the trees. The land dipped below her, clearly now in twilight, its ridges planed down, its rocks rubbed smooth. Nothing disturbed it. There was no truck parked by the stream; no one stood by the field gate. Her eyes searched down the valley. Nothing. Still peering, she thought something moved. Gradually it grew solid, took on a shape. Then she was running, tripping, sliding down the slope, flinging herself through the gateway and onto the road. She waved, shouted a greeting.

But the figure striding toward her was not Madge or a woman who might have been Greta, and however much Ren squinted, she could not squash this person smaller and reshape her into the boy.

Panic-stricken, she began to scramble back, but the traveler was calling; there were sounds that could be "stop" and "ask." Embarrassed by her childish flight, Ren waited.

When the stranger reached Ren, she demanded, "How far's the depot?"

"The depot?"

"Where the freight stops after checks."

Ren shook her head.

Exasperated, the girl clicked her tongue. "I've been walking all day and the only person I've seen gives me that for an answer! Where're you dug in?"

Ren pointed. "Behind those trees."

The girl looked up at them, then back at Ren, then up once more. She seemed to be calculating which was the less bearable: Ren or the coming rain. "I might as well stop off," she decided.

She was a street person! Ren was sure of that, from her clothes. They were a jumble of colors and textures and designs, piled on as if the girl's purpose was to transport her entire wardrobe. Ren could detect the cuffs of a blouse and the sleeves of a sweatshirt and a collar embroidered with beads; all these protruded at the borders of a hefty jumper. And there were the bottoms of pants under the hems of skirts, one of these edged with a fringe and another with a stripe of sackcloth; and a pair of boots of the kind soldiers wore on the story-screen; and over all these were a parka, a body vest, and a long plastic cape.

"After you," the girl said. "They're your quarters."

Ren scarcely noticed this respect for her territory. She was remembering what she had been taught: never to talk to any street person and to activate her screamer if one approached. Now here she was, alone with one of them, a girl taller than herself and almost certainly heavier, too, under the wads of clothes. And Ren was leading this person into her refuge. She tried to think up some excuse to stop her, but none came.

"Where's the tent, then?" the girl asked.

"There isn't one. I sleep in here." She stood aside for the girl to enter.

After the pause to adjust their eyes to the light, Ren watched the girl's head go around. She looked at the stack of cans, the sleeping bag screwed into a hump, the clothes scattered about, and pronounced, "It's a slum! You should bring in bracken. Makes decent matting. But you wouldn't know about that. There'll be proper carpets in your fancy residence."

Ren turned her face away, distressed by the girl's mockery of a home that was not at all fancy and whose carpets were threadbare.

"What're you doing here, anyway?" the girl demanded.

"I'm waiting for someone. She'll come get me any day. Perhaps tomorrow."

The girl scoffed, "Haven't you got feet at the end of your

legs?" but added, tugging off her boots, "Though, mind you, after the miles I've walked today, these things at the end of my legs don't feel like feet. More like a couple of raw flippers."

She removed the plastic cape, body vest, and parka, folded them, placed them on top of her knapsack, and laid out her sleeping bag. Before slipping into it, she drew something from a fold of a skirt. This she slid inside a pocket that was sewn into the bag. It was a knife.

Ren crept to her own bag and hid herself inside. She had longed to have someone beside her in the cave's darkness, but this was not the companion she had imagined. This one threatened, like all her kin.

The news-screens explained how they lived in empty houses where the water and electricity had been turned off, or they camped out-of-doors. They roamed and scavenged and were lawless savages. So from time to time the patrols had to go out and round them up. Her body tense, her palms clammy, Ren felt the probing night slink back and the menace of this girl slide into its place.

It had not withdrawn or permitted her to sleep when a voice whispered, "Are you awake?" Jerking, her hand protecting her throat, she wanted to cry out: "You can have the cave, keep all the supplies. I'll go and I won't tell anyone I've seen you. I promise." But the words would not come.

"Stop moaning," the voice continued. "It's only me. Come outside." Then she heard the snoring that came from the other sleeping bag, saw a deeper darkness shift from the cave opening, and she became aware of the faraway fluorescence of stars.

"Here," Brocket guided, and she found they were crouched by a stump of rock. "Is that other one still here?" he asked.

"How did you know she was with me?"

He hissed, impatient, "Saw. She's some walker. Better than the usual I see passing through, just bags of feeble muscle. Where's she headed?"

"The depot."

"I wouldn't be in her shoes if she's caught."

This sympathy was surprising. "Doesn't she scare you?"

"Why?"

"Being a street person, she . . ." Ren began, but there was too much to explain. Brocket had obviously never watched the news-screen.

"I'm not scared of *her*." He stressed the last word. "She wasn't the only one on the move tonight."

His words peopled the hills with watching eyes. She had disobeyed Madge's orders. This evening thoughtlessly she had rushed onto the road. Above her, the stars dimmed. "Are there patrolmen?"

"No, not them. Others. As a rule I give this place a wide berth nighttimes, only I was coming to you. Then I saw you bring that girl in. I waited a bit, to see if she stayed, and she did. So I said to myself: No need for you there tonight, Brocket; time to go back. It was getting dark. It was then I sensed someone else. I thought at first that it'd be someone attached to her, with a meeting lined up, but it wasn't anybody like that." His voice quavered and was barely audible. "It wasn't someone just *waiting, hanging about*. This one was on the hunt."

Ren was infected by his dread. Like Brocket, she could not speak the name of the giant Yordas. "But he didn't catch you," she whispered.

"He had my scent." He paused. "But I gave him the slip. I got up to the old cattle road, on the top, way above here. It was then that I found it. Dumped near the path."

"What? Dumped?"

"Like some do with dogs they don't want. Somebody must have pushed it up the track, the other side of the cliff, and it was parked under a hazel. By the side of one of the holes. Drop down there, and it'd be minutes before you hit anything. And when you did . . . I couldn't leave it, could I, the carriage thing? I had to bring it here."

"A carriage? What's the use of that?"

"It's what's inside it." For a moment his tone held a hint of apology. Ren waited. "A baby."

She was too astonished to answer. He tugged at what Ren had thought was a stump of rock behind them and there was the creak of a wheel.

"I couldn't just walk away from it, could I? He"—the boy gulped—"he, Yordas, would've got it. I can't take it back with me, either. He'll catch me, slowed down by this. I couldn't just leave it there, could I?" he repeated. "It'll be safe with you; *he* has no truck with girls."

She wanted to cling to him, to make him chant with her: Yordas can't harm us; it's centuries since he stalked over these hills; he is dead. But the shape she reached for had gone, its passage marked by the lift of leaves that rattled then sank again among the grass tufts. Yet her hand was not empty. It had found the buggy.

She shouted, "I can't take this!" but the shout was merely a whisper. For Brocket had not deserted the baby. Up there, on those night-soaked hills, among the bottomless holes, he had been haunted by a terror. Yet he had not run away.

What could she do with it?

What she could not do was clear: she could not tell her mother; she could not appeal to Madge, who had brought her to the cave; she had no screen that could give instructions on how to dispose of an abandoned child.

Beside her, the buggy trembled; there was a brief whimper, then stillness. Clumsily Ren turned the buggy toward her and looked under the hood. A head, cased in a woolen bonnet, lolled against the metal frame; a hand lay twitching slightly on the edge of a blanket.

Another thing she could not do was leave the child in the open. She fumbled with catches, straps, studs, a zipper, and at last the body was freed. It hung for a second from her arms' winch before landing against her chest. Gasping at the weight, she peered into the face. It was pale under the weak starlight; the eyes did not open to acknowledge her; the lips did not smile. For a moment Ren wavered; then, under the wrappings, a leg kicked and came to rest against her thigh. Ren turned, and carrying this surprising burden, she picked her way with the buggy around invisible rocks, through the drifts of leaves, and entered the lightless cave.

THREE

"I don't believe it!"

The girl was standing over her. Inside Ren's sleeping bag there was a lump and from it were coming inexplicable noises, deafening and shrill.

"I thought you'd got a crying doll. How did it get here?"

Confused, barely awake, Ren tried to sit up, to disentangle the baby. "Somebody left it."

"*Left it?* What do they think this is, a nursery?"

The baby was screaming, its mouth huge, its throat stretched. Incredulous that such a small creature could make such a great noise, Ren expected its lungs to explode and the rib cage to shatter in her hands. Only on the storyscreen had she watched anyone attend to a baby, and it was always pink and placid, not screeching and fiery red.

"Left it?" the girl repeated. "Who did?"

Ren shook her head. Brocket was her secret. She did not want to share him. No one else must know his fear of the cave's murderous ghost. This girl would be scornful of that, and she would batter Ren with questions. In fact, her sentences were rarely anything but questions. She was going on now, demanding to know the time the child had been deposited, the age, sex, and appearance of the "handler," the conditions and payment.

Using the cuff of her sweater, Ren dried the mucus from the baby's nose, but that annoyed it and it shrieked all the more. Shaking, she told the girl, "I found it outside."

The other stared. Then she leaned forward, looped her hands around the twisting body, and hoisted it out of Ren's grasp. "You poor waif," she murmured. "It's hungry," she told Ren, "but it'll have to wait a minute. I can't stand this smell."

Immediately she demanded ferns and dried leaves, laid the baby on them, peeled off the layers of pants and soiled diapers, and cleaned up. She would have sliced up a blanket to improvise a clean diaper; but Ren found some in the buggy. This had been carefully packed. The compartments at the sides and under the seat were filled with clothing and baby foods. There were extra supplies in bags tied to the handle.

"The one who dumped her was hoping she'd be picked up," the girl said. "As if, along here, there'd be much chance of anyone finding her!"

"I wonder what her name is."

"We'll call her Found."

Ren could think of more pretty names, but all she was able to contribute was: "Why?"

"She's not Lost, is she? Or Missing, Believed Dead. My

grandfather's grandpa was all of those. Found is more cheerful." It was impossible to deny that.

"Now I want a can of baby food opened, and be careful not to nick the spoon that'll be inside," the girl ordered.

Until that moment Ren had accepted her role of assistant. She had done as commanded and had watched, awed. For the girl was so skillful, her hands so deft and unhesitating, that not only did she appear totally sure of what she was doing but the baby seemed to know. She did not struggle; she reduced her screaming to an occasional sob; her color lost its vivid purple. But Ren considered herself capable of feeding her and, holding the can, asked, "May I do it?"

The girl frowned. "Not now. Having another person feed her could upset her. Babies get used to the one that looks after them. After she's eaten this," she said, taking the can, "I'll try her with the bottle. It's lucky the stuff in that thermos is still warm."

Ren wished the girl were a picture on the screen and could be removed at the push of a button. She imagined herself doing that. She looked at the girl, pinched her eyelids together, blinked, and the girl had gone! Cheered, she repeated the process. Unfortunately, however, this visitor came without your bidding and you could not dictate when she left. This street person was not an image; she had substance. She even snored.

"Now that she's burped, she'll settle," the girl announced. "Keep an eye on her while I slip out for a quick check."

The baby was peaceful, satisfied. Her eyelids quivered sleepily. A bubble formed at a corner of her mouth, broke, and saliva trickled to her chin. Tentatively, Ren wiped it away, whispering, "You won't be left by yourself again. I promise." She stretched out a finger, and a small fist closed over it. Gradually the hand relaxed, and Found sighed and slept.

Then the girl's voice hissed, "Listen. I'm off. There's trouble. Waiting. Down by the road."

"What is it? A patrolman?" Ren felt dizzy.

"Yes. Or a scout or one of the void officers in Security. You don't think I went close enough to see his number and unit, do you? I climbed up, top of here, to have a look around . . . and there he was. Down near the road. Sitting under a wall. I'm clearing out quick." She had already begun to roll up her sleeping bag.

"You might be caught."

"I'm leaving so I won't be! I reckon the truck driver, the one I hitched a lift from, must have reported me. I was told never to trust any of them. Curse him! I should have kept to my legs. But I'm not beaten so easily. There's the border in another hundred miles and I'm going to get over it. I'll not be run down here. There's no way out. It's a dead end." Her voice faltered. "I'd be penned in like a rat in a funnel."

Ren thought she would be sick. "Madge said none of them knows about this cave. Other people have stayed in it."

"Perhaps somebody's squealed." She muttered to herself, "Security have ways of making people." She was strapping her sleeping bag to her knapsack.

"But if the patrolman knows we're here, why doesn't he come and arrest us?"

"He'll have radioed for reinforcements. He'll wait till they come. You're on the run like me, aren't you?"

"Yes. My mother's expecting a baby."

"I guessed as much. Couldn't pay the tax, I suppose."

"No."

"It's more than a tax I'm running from. I suppose you

believe all that's given out on your news-screen. They don't mention that people die on the streets, and not only from hunger and cold." She zipped her parka.

"I don't know what to do."

The girl shrugged. "Depends what answers you've got when Security starts questioning."

Ren's breath left her. She had not been told to be prepared for questions. What would they be? What would be the right answers? What would happen if the answers were wrong? She thought of her mother and the new baby. Would they get into trouble? Agitated, confused, she wished there was someone who could help her. Then her eyes turned to Found.

"I'm going, then. If you take my advice, you won't linger," the girl urged. "Don't you know that if they catch you they'll stick you in a Surplus Children Unit?"

"Yes. My mother didn't want that. She said I'm not surplus." Wanly she repeated her mother's brave joke. "And neither is Found. What about her?"

The girl bit her lip. Then she said, her voice hoarse, "When the patrol moves in, they'll take her and the buggy. She'll be looked after."

Ren shook her head. Her hands trembling, she bent down, picked up a pebble, and added it to the two in her pocket.

"Look, above this cave there's good cover, plenty of trees," the girl told her. "I'll see you're all right as far as there."

"I'm not going. I'm staying with the baby."

"You're crazy!"

"She's been left once. It's not going to happen again."

"What good will it do if you stay?" Infuriated by Ren's obstinacy, she shouted. "You might as well walk out now and give yourself up."

"I'm not leaving her."

For a long moment the girl stood with her plastic cape draped over one shoulder, her knapsack ready at her feet, while she looked first at Ren and then at Found.

At length she sighed. "In that case, the baby'll have to come, too."

FOUR

They did not discuss the girl's decision. Ren murmured thanks while the other pretended that taking the baby had been her intention from the start. She introduced herself with, "I'm Lil. What about you?" They were getting down to business.

The first of that was a quick, gobbling breakfast. Then, "You pack your kit," Lil ordered, "and I'll choose the rations." But when everything was collected, it was clear that there was too much to carry on their backs. So they decided to put the heavier items in the buggy and take the baby in a sling. With Ren's nail scissors, Lil cut up a blanket, knotted on string that they found among the cave's supplies, and made the sling rainproof with a large plastic bag. They fitted the baby in it and hung it on Lil. One knapsack went on Ren's shoulders; the other and the sleeping bags were strapped on top of the provisions stacked in the buggy.

Lil crept out "to check on the enemy," reported that the man had not moved, and announced, "Okay. On your mark!"

They had worked so quickly that there had been no time to reflect on what they were doing and, ready to go, Ren hesitated. For a moment this hostile sanctuary was preferable to a journey with a street person and the dangers of an unknown region. But outside was a patrolman who would soon search for them, and a baby brought by Brocket and now slung from this street person's neck. She was already on the path, her silhouette bulbous with the full sling. Ren gripped the handle of the buggy, for the last time bobbed under the cave's arch, and felt the light of the early morning shimmer on her skin.

At first it seemed that they would never get up the path that led to the trees above the cave. Packing the carriage, they had not considered its weight.

"We could do with a winch," Lil said, trying to prevent the buggy from rolling down while Ren heaved. Eventually they simply unloaded it, carried it to the top, ferried the goods up to it, and repacked. That done, they had to hump it around rocks and fallen branches, through leaves and deep grass that caught in the wheels. The task seemed beyond their strength, but they could not give up. Their thoughts were slanted toward the valley where the patrolman waited.

Finally, when the trees were behind them, they reached a terrace and turned up a path. This must be the old cattle road Brocket came by, Ren thought. It ran almost level, but the buggy kept tilting into the ruts and had to be heaved out. So, hoping to find easier going, they took a pathway downward and entered the road.

"I walked along here yesterday," Lil said, "and now I'm tramping back! But we won't meet any truck that the patrolman may have radioed for. They can't get a vehicle along this road."

Ren wondered whether she would ever get the buggy along it. Rain and frost had broken up its surface, which was crumbling and full of holes. Also, it rose steeply, and as Ren pushed the buggy she worked yard by yard, her muscles straining for each upward thrust.

She did not know how far they traveled. She did not see the streams stitching through the bracken, the distant mountains, the collapsed field walls. Then, when they descended into another valley and she was forced to tug at the buggy as it swept downward, she did not notice how the land had changed. Her focus was on the buggy, on the pain in her back and neck. Until she heard Lil say, "Time for a rest."

Leaning her arms on the handle of the buggy, Ren looked up and saw that the hills around her were green and silken. Shrubs and trees red with berries were rooted among the rubble of walls.

"There's an old barn in that field." Lil pointed, and Ren stumbled after her. "The roof's fallen down at that end, but it's dry over here. Now, where's the baby food?"

Ren had a memory of helping to search for it, of Found sucking fiecely at the bottle, her fingers gripping Lil's wrist. She heard Lil say, "I reckon we can lay our heads down for a bit." Then she dropped into a corner and felt the scratch of straw.

They did not sleep long. Found's crying woke them. "She's hungry again," Lil announced unnecessarily. "When she's finished all the feed in that thermos, we'll have to scout for water to make up more."

"I have to go outside," Ren told her. It seemed years since she had sat in a proper lavatory. "Do you suppose it's safe?"

"Well, you're not doing it in *here*. You won't be seen by the wall. Visibility's poor at dusk."

Probably for that reason and because she was not fully awake, Ren did not see the mound of clothes until she stumbled into it. And it said, "Careful now. You should wait till you've found your night eyes."

Ren cried out and would have run, but twig fingers, their roots in matted mittens, latched over her belt.

"Now, now, there's no need for silliness. You think I'm a witch, don't you? Well, have I a wart on my nose or a pointed hat or a broomstick? Have I got a cat? Here, Puss! Puss!" The old woman cackled. "Like it says in your storybooks."

Ren dared not tell her that there were no books in the living-work units; they were deemed unnecessary, since the tenants were provided with a complete bank of screens. But while the story-screen had often had pictures of witches on it, to Ren's surprise she discovered that they had missed something: they gave no hint of the smell. This old woman's came from her filthy clothes and gushed on her breath: frowsty, sweaty, rank with the stink of animals and moldering earth. Ren felt stifled.

"How did you know we're here?"

"I don't have a telephone or one of those picture machines, but there isn't much I miss." She released Ren's belt and folded her arms, complacent. "I knew there was only you to start with, a poor chick shoveled out of its nest, and I learned there was an infant in the party before I heard its noise."

"Who told you?"

"You won't get an answer, less I see fit. It's best to keep your secrets. Take my advice on that."

"Yes," Ren agreed, wanting to get away from this old woman. "You'll have to excuse me."

"By all means; it's natural. But I'd not squat by those nettles. They'll sting your bottom."

This was embarrassing. "I meant, I ought to be helping Lil."

"It's about time I had a look at this baby," the old woman said, and followed Ren to the entrance of the barn.

Found was sitting in the buggy drumming her heels and watching Lil pour her food from the thermos into the bottle.

"We've got a visitor," Ren warned her.

Seeing the stranger, Lil stiffened and a hand scrambled under the layers of clothing as if making a search.

"She heard us come."

"Funny we didn't hear her," Lil said, keeping her eyes on the woman.

"She would need bat ears to catch a whisper of me," the woman addressed the baby. Startled, Found turned her head and examined the stranger.

"What do you want?" Lil demanded.

"Now isn't she the edgy one? But we mustn't blame her. It's the way she's had to live," the woman confided to Found. "We know about her kind, don't we? I've met one or two. Prime fellows they were, but I couldn't put up with some of their practices. So you tell her that if it's a knife she's rummaging for, she can save herself the trouble. I'm only here to see how you thrive, and you don't appear to be doing so badly, all things considered. Nevertheless, you'll be growing tired of those cans. I've brought you a drink of the best."

Opening her coat, she unhooked a can from her belt. A white liquid dribbled over its sides.

"What's that?" Lil intervened.

"Better than anything there is in those containers." She creaked down and peered into the child's smooth face. Her own was wrinkled and dry; there was a fringe of hairs around the lips that murmured: "Your nursemaids aren't happy with this, I can tell, but it's for you to decide. You'll like it; it's got more body than that thin stuff they're giving you, and it's still warm, straight from the teat." She unscrewed the lid of the can, poured some of the milk into it, and cupping the small head in her palm, she pushed it against the rim. For a moment Found resisted; she tucked her lips together and drew back. But, feeling the splash of liquid, she frowned, extended an adventuring tongue, and licked. Interested, she stretched her neck, made a slit of her mouth, and opened her throat to an experimental trickle. "No matter if it catches your breath," the old woman soothed as the baby spluttered. "It's a bit on the strong side for a little one, but you won't taste anything better."

Found may not have agreed, but after a gasp and a cough, she locked her gums over the side of the lid and, her feet pounding, her shoulders jerking to the rhythm of snorting gulps, she drank.

"What was that?" Lil asked again, her voice loud. All the time the baby had been taking the drink, she had been trying to prevent it, had tried to make a grab, but the woman had held her off. Now she pounced, heaved, and with the child held tightly against her, she shouted, "You shouldn't interfere. Keep out of the way! Who are you, anyway? Barging in and pouring stuff down her. And look at her now! It must be poisonous. She's going to be sick."

For the baby's expression had become intense; her cheeks swelled and strained.

"Little she knows about infants, but you'll teach her, won't you?" The woman still spoke to Found. "Only, I suppose she'd rather not notice you're filling your britches. Give her something to do, the ungrateful hussy." She rose. Dignified but trembling, she continued, "You just tell her Annie Gimmer doesn't go about serving poison to little ones. It's been a pleasure meeting you, my beauty, but I don't think I'll visit again."

"You aren't invited."

The woman ignored her. "To be truthful, I wouldn't have bothered. I've enough to do tending myself; but I promised to see how you are doing, little one, and I can see you're healthy. I wish you all the luck the good spirits dole out. You'll need it."

"Who did you promise?" But Lil received no answer. Annie Gimmer had gone.

"Do you know what the old crone was going on about, Ren?"

She shook her head. She was thinking, The old woman called herself Annie Gimmer; Brocket had mentioned her; he said she had walked the drovers' ways and had tales to tell.

She could see that Annie Gimmer had stopped a little distance from the barn. A slight wind ruffled her garments until, discovering that the thin body offered no resistance, it grew bold and began to snatch.

"You hurt her feelings," Ren rebuked Lil, and could not believe her daring.

"Some chance of that!"

Watching the old woman, Ren saw her head sag; a sleeve was inched up and was wiped across the face. Then, bent as if she carried a crippling load, she began to walk toward the lane. "I have to go after her."

"Don't be a fool. She knows something. She knows this baby was dumped."

"She only wanted to help."

"Ren, folks like her are hard-bitten, really tough."

And how do you describe yourself and the street people? Ren asked silently.

"You've a lot to learn."

"I know. I keep being told." Tramps were never seen near the living-work units, so Ren had no one to compare Annie with. It was difficult to judge for herself. Her body was heavy with weariness; her stomach was a hollow cavern echoing with memories of food; her brain did not seem to be contained in her head but had floated away. She stepped over the cracked threshold. "I've got to go to her."

"Ren! Be careful." Lil's voice was shrill as it followed her. "She could be in the pay of Security. She'd be useful, passing on the whereabouts of people she's sighted."

"You said the milk was poisonous."

"She stinks."

Her mind clear for a moment, Ren called back, "And so do we."

FIVE

Although Annie Gimmer's pace was slow, Ren found it difficult to catch up with her. Her legs were stiff and unwieldy; her arms would not swing. The emptiness in her stomach did not make her body lighter, but more cumbersome. "I've come to apologize," she practiced and did not know she was repeating the sentence out loud until she heard, "Have you?" and discovered the other had halted.

"Yes. Lil shouldn't have said that."

"Are those your words, or hers?" To Ren's silence, she answered, "I thought so. I would be more forgiving if it was her that put herself out."

"She didn't mean it."

Annie Gimmer stared until Ren blushed at the lie. Satisfied, she observed, sympathetic, "I can see you need nourishment. You come along with me."

"I have to stay hidden. A patrolman might see me."

"Not here. There's none of their breed traveling this valley on this autumn evening."

So Ren walked with Annie Gimmer down the narrow lane. The twilight was deepening, but she could see they were passing cottages. Grass whiskered the sills and the doorsteps. At the holes where stone tiles had slipped down, the roof beams were exposed.

"Doesn't anyone live there?" she asked.

"Not permanent. They're handy for travelers and strays. Now and again you'll find a place done up. What they call a holiday residence."

There was a larger building that Ren supposed must have once been a farm. By the door was a small boxlike construction, which she knew from cartoons was a kennel for dogs. A chain curled out of it. Nearby was a low shed. "What's that?"

"Cow parlor it was. That's all done away with. The cattle aren't here anymore. With the sort of rearing there is nowadays, they can be kept just as well on the spot, in town factories."

"Is that why everyone is gone?"

"Mostly. Folk can't live on air." She laughed. "Though I give it a good try."

Still pegged to a clothesline was a child's woolen hat. It was shrunken and matted; the thread in its tassel had been plucked by inquisitive beaks. Looking at it, Ren thought she would cry.

"A few have stayed," Annie Gimmer was telling her, "where they can eke out enough to get by. And you'll still see sheep near the hilltops, which means shepherds, one or two."

They had reached a cluster of sheds and the litter of

farming tools gnawed by rust. Behind was a stone barn. The old woman led Ren to it. Under what remained of the roof was a manger lined with straw and a metal pot balanced on glowing embers.

"Sit you down," Annie Gimmer ordered.

It was a delicious meal Ren ate there. Later she was told that the meat was rabbit that Annie Gimmer had snared. The thick, unleavened biscuit had been cooked at the edge of the woman's improvised hearth. "I call it my backstone. I don't choose to use the kitchen." She pointed toward the farm. "An empty house has echoes, and they're jealous of their rights. I keep to the barns, where I can see sky. They were always my lodging, when I was a traveling woman."

"Brocket told me."

Annie Gimmer nodded, showing no surprise. "He's not a bad lad. He's shaping up, a credit to his nurture, though I shouldn't say it, since it was me brought him up."

Ren thought, Then why does he call her *Mrs.* Gimmer? It was too formal. She asked, "Where has he gone?"

"Who can say? He'll come if he's hungry. There's no telling when he'll turn up."

Ren agreed. "When he brought the baby, he came in the middle of the night!" She added, "Last night," surprised because it seemed so far away.

Annie Gimmer nodded. "The young rapscallion keeps unchristian hours. But it seems what he did was sensible, and I've done as promised: I've had a squint at the babe. There's naught else I can offer. I'm past fostering." She took Ren's plate and smiled to see it was polished clean. "Now that you've got food inside you, it's time you were off."

Obedient, Ren got up. "I don't know where I should be off to. Someone is after us; Lil says we're being tracked down.

And now there's the baby." Suddenly she was confiding, describing how she came to be in that valley, how the arrangement had gone wrong. She forgot her weariness; she lost her timidity; she was unaware of any effort to talk. The words came nudging, jostling, and then hurtling off her tongue until everything had been said.

"My goodness, what a tale! I must say you were a brave little creature in that cave, sticking it out by yourself." The wrinkles crisscrossing her face became delicate shadows when she smiled. "Since you can do that, I'd judge there's not much that'll beat you."

Ren blushed at the compliment. "But now Madge won't know where to look for me."

"She'll manage; and just you remember what your mother said. She wasn't telling stories. Where that Greta lives is a nice place for a young one. So my advice is set course for her."

"I don't know the name of the service station."

"You can unriddle that in due time, when you've given the hunting one the slip. That's first. Since you're certain there's somebody stalking." Her eyes left Ren and focused beyond her, among the tumbledown sheds. "I'll have to do some considering."

"Will you help us?"

"I'll think on it, haven't I said?" Her voice rose, suddenly peevish. "I'm not so young as I was. I can't be marching over these hills with two young girls on the run and a mite in arms. But you're a good one, not above yourself like that other. So you do as you're bid and stay in that barn till I've worked out what's to be done with you. Now make yourself scarce."

"Thank you for the stew." She remembered to be polite

although the old woman's hand was over her elbow, pinching her to go. "I should have kept some. Lil would have enjoyed it."

In answer, Annie Gimmer scraped out the pot onto a tin plate.

"I didn't say that in order to scrounge some more," Ren protested.

"Then you should have. What words I've exchanged with that bossy boots is no matter. She has a sharp tongue on her, but she's to be praised, the way she tends that child."

Ren nodded. She would have described the thoroughness of Lil's care, but the hand on her elbow had begun to push and she was being steered out of the barn.

On the lane, Ren looked back and waved. The woman merely flapped a hand, dismissing her. Ren thought: I wish she hadn't bustled me out so quickly. Still, she said she would "do some considering," so perhaps she will help me find Greta. And as she entered the barn that thought made her smile.

"You've taken your time," Lil greeted. "Steering clear of the mess and the bother of getting the baby down. And watch your noise. I don't want her woken up."

"I wouldn't do that."

"What's that stuff you're carrying?"

"Rabbit stew. It's better than anything."

"If it's come from that old hag, you can chuck it."

"I brought it specially for you."

"Well, I might force it down." Lil relented, seeing Ren's face.

Handing the plate to her, Ren noticed what Lil had done. She had removed the contents from Ren's knapsack and arranged them on the barn floor. Ren stared, not knowing how to challenge or to object.

"This looks like a neat gadget," Lil commented. She held up Ren's dental groomer.

"You can have it." Perhaps Lil envied these possessions. "Take anything you want."

"I'm fitted out okay, but I wouldn't say you are."

"It wasn't expected that I'd be going on a long hike."

Lil laughed and replaced Ren's belongings in the knapsack. "That's that. Just a routine search."

Ren decided not to ask her what she'd been searching for. She wanted to tell her that Annie Gimmer had promised to help them; she wanted to report that the old woman had not seen a patrolman that morning.

But her tongue would not work, and it was difficult to see Lil through the gauze of approaching sleep. Words were heard indistinctly: "can't be sure we've shaken him off," and "move on tonight."

Then later there was crying, the baby smells of food and diapers. After that, still drowsy, she was hauled into a sitting position and the child thrust onto her lap. She heard, "We'll strike camp when I've finished scouting. There should be a village not far away, near where I got off the truck. The driver said it was empty. Now that it's dark, I can check."

A plastic cape crackled; skirts swirling round trousers created a draft; within the barn's opening, a shape was profiled against the night sky and the voice breathed: "Found's decided she wants a good whine, but you'll have to quiet her or else she'll be heard."

And if she was, who might arrive to investigate? Ren asked the empty barn. Would a patrolman appear at the door, swing the beam of his flashlight across the dirt floor and along the walls until it found the baby struggling in Ren's arms and with its blinding light pinned them both down? Or would it be a creature? One whose ears would catch the sound of Found's miserable crying, which would not stop, however much Ren jogged and rocked. This beast would come sniffing, as the boy had feared, for he knew what fanged things prowled in the darkness, what giants strode from their caves, what ogres sprang from the gullies. In the deserted homesteads, Annie had felt the spirits lingering; their peace broken, they would seek out this noise.

But there was nothing Ren could do to silence Found. Her soothing whispers were not heard above the interminable wails. As if she, too, sensed danger, the baby's screams grew more desperate; her chest bubbled, her feet kicked, and she thrashed to escape the restraint of Ren's grasp. Together they wrestled, while the terrors of the night gathered, invisible.

There were noises. Paws scratched along the rafters. Ren's head jerked up; she saw the hole in the roof. It contracted. A mass leaned over the edge. Now it was her throat that shrieked.

"Who's there? Mrs. Gimmer, is that you? Mrs. Gimmer! Mrs. Gimmer!"

The scraping hands vanished and the head that had poked under the roof beam was there no more.

Ren listened for the skid of boots down the wall, the thud of them descending on the grass, but no sounds reached her above Found's noise. No one could have climbed up there, she told herself. There was nobody. It was just a bad dream.

She managed to loosen her frantic grip on the baby. She hauled her up to rest against her shoulder and pillowed the head in her palm. "Nothing and no one shall ever harm you,

I promise. I won't let it," she murmured. What had Annie Gimmer said? "There's not much that'll beat you."

She was encouraged by the memory; her body became less tense and, feeling this, Found relaxed. Hooped in the sanctuary of Ren's arms, she gradually grew quiet while Ren, steady and alert, stared into the night.

SIX

There was no mistaking the next noises; they crackled the silence that had bound her while the baby slept. Again panic sluiced through Ren as a stone rattled, as a weight thumped, but she could not escape, make a rush for the doorway with the child tight on her lap. She heard the scrape of a zipper being opened, a series of impatient scratches, then saw, within the tent of a cape, the swaying leaf of a flame.

"Are you awake?" Lil asked. In the light of the match, her eyes were bloodshot and shadows pooled her cheeks.

Choked by relief, Ren could not answer.

"I came upon these." Plunder tumbled from her parka: a toy, a cup, candles, a bundle of white toweling, but her voice was not triumphant. "We'll be glad of the matches. Now we have to leave. Quick."

"Has someone seen you?"

"Seen me? I can case a joint without being seen." However, the boast quivered.

"There was . . . I thought there was, a person, up there on the roof. I'm not sure." Ren could not disentangle the sensations; she could not separate the nightmare of the prowling creatures from the huge poking head.

"There's someone around." The flame shrank along its stalk. "In one of the cottages . . . there were . . . ashes in the hearth . . . a pan with food in it . . . hadn't had time to grow mold. We have to hurry."

"Perhaps he heard Found crying."

"I'll strike another match while you pack the carriage."

"I couldn't stop her."

"It probably made no difference," Lil whispered, and Ren was grateful to her for not apportioning blame.

Lil did not because during her search she had discovered that she herself was not perfect. But pride kept her silent. What she had done had broken the rules of her training, and she was ashamed.

Lil was accustomed to danger, but she had never before undertaken that kind of venture alone. Always she had been accompanied; it was a rule that when you went on a raid you worked in a team. Guards and lookouts were necessary, for if street people were caught, they had no rights by law. How they were dealt with depended on whim. Yet this night Lil had ignored everything she had been taught. She had calculated that if the man following them was in one of the houses, she would discover him before he saw her, and she would be able to escape.

Even so, she had been frightened. She was not used to

night in the country. Roofed by trees, the lane to the village was a tunnel lit neither by street lamps nor by stars. Lil blundered onto its grass shoulders and cried out at the sudden thrust of a low, searching branch. When, later, her feet slid and stumbled, she thought she walked upon large pebbles until she realized they were cobblestones, and as the sky cast a faint sheen upon them, she saw that at last she was in the village street.

Relieved, she leaned against a house wall. "I've walked faster than I thought," she told herself, because she did not want to admit it was fear that had caused the trickles of sweat. But these dried up as soon as she began to explore. In this kind of terrain Lil was confident, a skilled pirate.

She was very thorough. Plotting her own points of reference—a flight of scooped steps, a projecting sill, an iron gate—she worked systematically, section by section, covering every house. Now assisted by stars and the moon-hinting sky, she peered, listened, felt, her hands examining doorjambs, her fingers probing the frames of windows, and she discovered that, although she had brought her tools, she would not need to employ them. The windows and doors were not locked.

Lil peered at the knob that had just turned in her hand, shocked and confused. For she had never experienced anything like this: houses left open, almost welcoming those without shelter. Usually property was heavily guarded, if not with guns and alarms, then with chains, padlocks, wire, bolts. This door inching open frightened her. The cottage had grown sinister. Squeezing herself against the clean-cut stone, she heard her breath scrape. Her heart drummed.

Eventually she slid her knife out of a pocket, and holding it firmly in her palm, she stepped inside. With her ears stretched like muscles straining for an object beyond reach, she listened to the silence. It hammered its way into her head. There it swelled and grew into rhythmic thuds like the stamp of boots, bringing with them the rattle of guns. Gasping, Lil threw back her arm and swung down the knife in a strong, curving downstroke. But there were no boots or bullets in that cottage. The knife had sliced through empty air.

And its path had run through starlight that laid a feathery illumination at her feet. It showed her a low shelf on which rested matches and candles. Still trembling with the menace that had invaded her head, Lil grabbed, fumbled; a flame gushed and was transferred to a candle's wick. In its light she saw varnished flagstones, a scraggy mattress, a cone of neatly chopped wood beside an iron hearth, a saucepan crusted with soot. There was nothing strange about any of these. The cottage was simply a place used by tramps. What did surprise her was a collection of things arranged tidily on a piece of old cloth: a baby's teething ring, a soft toy so worn that it was impossible to know what it was, a cup, a carton of powdered milk, and squares of white toweling, individually folded, which Lil recognized as old-fashioned diapers. Crooning with satisfaction, Lil tightened the belt of her parka, opened the zipper, and stuffed her haul into its capacious pouch.

It was only then that Lil saw the oatmeal in the saucepan and the heavy spade propped by the hearth. And the quiet cottage was filled with noises again. She heard the ring of the pan dropped onto the flagstones as she imagined the owner leaping to face her; she saw him grasp the spade's wooden handle, saw it lift above her shoulder, and heard the crack as the blade sliced through the bone.

She blew out the flame. The spiral of smoke was invisible, but she could smell the melted wax. "Why ever did I light it?" she whispered. "I forgot the danger! The window has no curtain. I could've been seen for miles."

Then she was out of the cottage, her feet tripped by a boot scraper and twisted in the holes of the crumbling lane. To the rhythm of her rasping breath, the thought panted: They mustn't find me; I mustn't be caught. But she was anxious about more than her own safety. If she was captured, there would be a search, and Ren and the baby would be discovered, too. Because of her folly. She had broken the code of her people. Lil groaned at the disgrace.

Now, groping over the floor of the barn, she collected the spilled booty and argued to herself that at least she had won this.

"What about Mrs. Gimmer?" Ren asked her. "She said we were to wait. I think she was going to help me reach Greta."

"Well, she's too late. Anyway, we'll be going in the general direction, more or less south. I'll take the buggy this time, and you carry Found."

"I'd like to do that."

However, Lil's offer had nothing to do with giving Ren pleasure. She could not risk carrying Found herself. That would hinder swift action. You need speed and agility for defense.

SEVEN

Partially roused as she was laid in the sling, the baby agitated them both by her whimpering distress. But snug against Ren's chest and lulled by her movements, Found curled inside her warm hammock and went back to sleep. Then Ren became aware of her load. It pulled on her neck and made her shoulders ache. However, she vowed that she would not complain. In a way, she thought later, she was lucky to have other things to consider.

In the darkness of the lane, she was no better at sensing her way than Lil had been earlier, but she put one hand beside Lil's on the buggy and used that as a guide.

"The truck driver dropped me somewhere along here, I think," Lil whispered, "so I'm hoping we're on the road I came by. I won't be sure till I see the river. Is that you?"

"What?"

"That noise? Hold it."

They stopped, but could hear nothing.

"Listen."

"Is it Found?" Ren suggested as the child's breath suddenly whistled.

"No. It's under the trees. If anyone jumps out, you lie down. I don't want to be punching the wrong one. So stay clear. Safe."

Safe! Ren thought, I haven't been safe since I left home. Now she and Lil were not only in flight but had to be ready for ambush. "What did you do, Lil?" she whispered.

"*Do?* I didn't do anything. I'm a street person. That's enough. Scum. Security are after you on the streets, and yet they'll not let you be if they find you trying to get out. It's their way of enjoying themselves."

"I see." Ren asked no more questions. She was thinking, When they did reports on the news-screen about street people, they never said anything like that.

They had not walked far before the nature of the darkness changed. Low by the roadside it distilled into mist.

"It's the river," Lil whispered. It guided them forward, steamed under them when they crossed over it, and continued at their side.

"That's the two bridges. I remember them. In a mile or two there should be a railroad track. We'll walk down it."

"What about the trains?"

"The truck driver told me the line's been closed for years."

"I seem to be seeing more," Ren murmured later.

"Soon be dawn."

It came gently. Hunched over their burdens, they watched the surface of the lane become pale, grow level and smooth for their surer steps. Beside them, the steam sheeting the river slunk under branches and showed them water foamed by boulders and sliding over great slabs of rock. They saw a post with a point, a swelling, gray, a stirring, feathers—a bird. It rose heavily, flapped broad wings, and led their eyes upward over the trees and into the opal sky.

And they saw in the distance a line of arches. Massive yet slender, they hoisted the sky's weight with ease upon their huge shoulders and windowed the light.

"What is it?" Ren asked.

"A viaduct. For the railway."

"I can't walk on top of that! I just can't," Ren said. She was hungry; pain screamed in her neck; her legs were buckling. And she could look no longer. Turning her eyes away, she confessed, "I'll be dizzy. I'll fall off."

"You'll steady up after a rest," Lil stated, briskly. "We'll stop off under those trees," and without further deliberation, she left the road, leading Ren across a field and into a small wood.

Ren saw no significance in Lil's quick decision. As she mixed Found's food, using water Lil had taken from the river, and as she opened cans for themselves, all she could think of was sleep. She made no comment when Lil announced, "Before it's fully daylight I'll scout around. Join you two for a quick nap when I come back."

Lil was pleased not to be questioned. There's no proof I spotted it, she argued to herself. A head, shoulders, above the parapet of the viaduct, the minute Ren looked away. Her telling about a head poking through the barn roof has started me seeing visions. With a line around the head, perhaps the hard brim of a cap. It could've been a mirage like Great-great-grandpa met when he was soldiering in the desert.

Lil hoped that it was a mirage, because if the watcher was the man pursuing them, it was her fault he was there. He could have seen her light in the cottage. He could have gone ahead of her to the barn and frightened Ren. Then, afterward, all he had to do was wait until they came out and follow them.

Why doesn't he catch up and try to arrest us? she asked wearily. I'd welcome a straight fight.

Refreshed by a short nap after her breakfast, the baby soon woke Ren. Shoulders throbbing, sleep misting her eyes, she groped for the buggy and lifted the baby out. Immediately, the wailing ceased. Ren was flattered. Perhaps she could even learn how to play with her. She sat Found on the sleeping bag and, after tickling her in the ribs, wondered what to do next. Preoccupied, she did not see Brocket until he stood beside her.

He grinned at her sharp cry. "You've got a frog's jump!"

"How did you know we were here?"

"Looked." He returned the baby's stare. "What sort is it, then?"

"A girl. We call her Found."

"Look at that sticking-out chin. Aren't girls supposed to be pretty?"

"She is. More than I am." Ren was sorry she had said that. It might prompt the boy to think that she was ugly.

He examined her dispassionately. "I don't think so. I like your brown eyes and you'll look better with all your side teeth. There's not much more I can see under the dirt."

"Who's talking!"

"Dirt's useful. I leave this on for camouflage." Seeing Ren

stroke a shoulder when she laughed, he asked, "Was she heavy in that sling?"

"You bet. Try her."

Brocket put out his hands, paused, and quickly jammed them back into his pockets. "She might cry," he excused himself. "Look, I've fetched her some milk. Mrs. Gimmer's boiled it, she says you're to know. So it keeps longer."

"She gave me a dish of stew yesterday."

"Rabbit or partridge?"

"Rabbit."

"I can't decide which I like best." He sighed, dreaming. "Only she'd run out of stew this morning."

Ren did not like to confess that she and Lil had been given the last of it. "I wish I could have stew at Mrs. Gimmer's every day."

"I don't have it every day. I used to live with her all the time, but I don't anymore. Here, I brought these."

He held out a twist of fabric. On it Ren saw soft globes each made of tiny beads that were polished and fat. Some had split and oozed a magenta juice.

"What are they?"

His mouth gaped. "You don't know? Blackberries. Try a taste."

Hesitantly, she took one, rolled it over her tongue, and squashed it warily between her teeth. "That's lovely." Her eyes filled. Once it had been her mother who had given her small treats. "May I have another?"

" 'Course. There's plenty more by the river. Would she fancy one?"

"The seeds might stick in her throat."

"Her throat's as wide as this valley! I've heard her yell." But he deferred to Ren's caution, and pressing two of the berries in his palm, he produced a rich syrup. "Here, have a lick of this," he commanded, and pushed the tip of a finger against Found's lips. She sucked it in, accepted it again, then, her nostrils flaring with disgust, she opened her mouth and let the juice drip away.

"She's quick to show her mind on a matter," he said, admiring. Then Found leaned forward and emitted a long, growling fart.

"Just listen to that!" Brocket exclaimed, delighted. But Found had not finished. She had at her command a whole arsenal, some small shot rattling out, some fast, bursting grenades, and after tense seconds of waiting as the flame on the fuse raced toward the gunpowder, a deep rumbling explosion. Brocket knelt beside her and, puffing out his face, attempted to compete. Until at last Found lost interest, drew her performance to a close with a modest hiss, and yawned. As they stopped laughing, the boy said, "She could teach Mrs. Gimmer a thing or two," and Ren told him, "Lil's coming."

Brocket rose. "I nearly forgot!" He began to unfasten the buckles on his pack and paid no attention to Lil until, reaching him, she demanded, "Who're you?"

"I could ask the same."

She regarded him, judged his power and weight, calculated that her own were superior, and drew her hand out of her pocket, empty. "How did you get here?"

"Walked. There isn't much call for buses in these parts."

"What do you want?"

"Will you lay off?"

"You might do jobs for Security."

The boy's lips flickered. "They wouldn't be interested. I

don't own one of those!" He pointed to her pocket where she kept the knife.

Lil flinched. "Curse you. Who told you I did?"

"Mrs. Gimmer warned me it wouldn't be a hankie you'd stretch for."

"Her? That old witch? You're in with her?" Her lips tight, it seemed that Lil might leap at him and squeeze his throat in her fists.

Ren intervened: "Mrs. Gimmer sent him. With more milk for—"

"So he's her errand boy." The scorn was corrosive.

"No. I'm her son. Adopted. Just watch your mouth."

"And what's happened to hers?" Lil shrieked, pointing at Found. Without turning her back on the boy, she slid over to Found and tilted the baby's face. "What's this on her chin?" Then she saw the juice-sodden rag and the few remaining berries. For a moment she was rendered speechless, before: "You fools. You ignorant, dim-witted, clod-headed fools. Pushing blackberries on her! Raw! She's a baby, not an experiment. How would you like it if someone stuffed a handful of blackberries in your mouth?"

"We didn't. It was only the juice," Ren stuttered.

"I wouldn't say no," the boy told her. "Save me the trouble of picking them. Now if you've got a minute, I'll hand this over." Opening his knapsack, he pulled out a small box and swung it by the handle set into the lid. In each of the sides was a pane of crystalline material that looked brittle and was yellowed with smoke. Behind these was a candle. "You light it through this little door," he instructed.

"Don't teach me how to light a lantern!" Lil snapped.

"Mrs. Gimmer sent it. 'And you tell them,' she said, 'my advice is go through the tunnel.'"

"Why?"

"Ask her. I'm only the errand boy."

Ren said, "I don't want to go by a tunnel." She imagined it, a pipe resounding with footsteps that ceased when you paused to listen but started immediately when you walked on.

Lil, too, appeared to have her own fears. Her mood had changed; her hostility was suspended. She stared away from the boy and stood taut, her fingers twisting the fabric of a skirt. "A tunnel's a death trap. There's no escape. You can be picked off as you come out. I didn't ask for advice."

"You don't have to take it."

"It could be a trick."

"Mrs. Gimmer's not one to play tricks. You've got traps and tricks on the brain."

"I have cause."

For a moment he was silent, then said quietly, "You'd not be seen in the tunnel."

That was true, but Lil moaned, "I hadn't planned on a tunnel."

Or viaducts. She regarded the boy. Would she have seen his head so far away? He was not wearing a cap, but he may have tucked that out of sight. Was he the person who had been spying on them? Carefully she composed a question: "Do you ever walk along it, the viaduct?"

"You wouldn't catch me on that! It's years since it was looked after. I reckon any moment it could come crashing down."

He had found nothing suspicious about the question. Lil thought, He wasn't lying; it wasn't this one that was up there behind the parapet this morning.

She said, "When I've fitted in a nap, we might give that tunnel a try." She tried to ignore Ren's frightened face.

"Do you want to know a shortcut to it?" He pointed through the trees, described landmarks: a waterfall, a ruined farmhouse, a bridge. "Then you'll see the railroad track and the cutting. That leads straight to the tunnel." Brocket paused, wanting to encourage them, but all he could add was, "You'll manage. I've brought you a lantern. That means it won't be as bad as walking down the tunnel in the dark."

He knew that the words didn't sound as hopeful as he had intended, and he saw the girls flinch.

EIGHT

Brocket sat by the entrance to the tunnel, not too close and hidden by shrubs. He wanted to be sure they followed his directions correctly, but he had not calculated that he would have to wait all morning; he had forgotten that Lil had planned to take a nap.

There were other things he could be doing, he rebuked himself. He could be picking more blackberries or checking on Mrs. Gimmer's snares. He could not lay them himself: he could not deliberately set out to catch a rabbit; but if one was caught and not wriggling too much, he would take it, find Mrs. Gimmer, and hang around till it was cooked.

"You're not trying to save my legs but fill your belly," she would scold, and she was right. "Now you buzz off," she would say when he had eaten, "and go for a walk."

He did so because he would not impose on her. Had she

not found him right at the start? Fed him and taught him some of her lore? He had told Ren that someone had dumped Found as people dump dogs they grow tired of, but she was not the first baby that had been dumped.

In a moment he would crawl from this hiding place and have a look around. He had not undertaken to do that; they were not expecting him to be standing guard, but he had decided he should. He suspected that this was no ordinary chase.

There had been something peculiar about it right from the start. It worried him.

He selected a pinecone and placed it between his feet. "That's the baby where I picked her up. It's a mystery who left her in that particular place. Next morning there's a patrolman down on the road and Ren and Lil bolt with her out of the cave." He moved the cone an inch.

"But the man didn't go after them and catch them. That's the second mystery. He had chances enough.

"Questions: Why didn't he pounce? Why didn't he corner them in the barn?" Brocket scraped at the earth, laid the cone in the nest he had made, and dangled a twig over it.

"There's another thing. Why haven't I seen him? He's a good tracker. Better than me," Brocket admitted, and covered the twig with leaves.

It was time to do a check. He inched on his belly to the top of the cutting and crouched in the protection of a hazel bush whose leaves yellowed the grass. He examined the ground thoroughly. A good distance away, the slopes of the mountain showed nothing unusual; behind him he could make out no watching shape among the crags. Beneath him, driven deep through the granite rock, was the tunnel.

Brocket held his breath, listening. The decayed branch

of a sycamore creaked, rooks flapped, but the sounds that came to his ears from the tunnel's dark mouth were the clang of alarm bells, the screech of tearing timbers, the thud of crashing rocks, the cries that shrilled before they were stifled by the black foaming dust.

"That didn't stop the building of it," Mrs. Gimmer had said. "They opened the tunnel up again and dragged the men out. Then they placed them in tidy graves. But that didn't stop them from wandering. It was a bad death they had, and they rise up and go back where they ended, to mourn. You can hear them. The groans and lamentations. By those that keep them in memory, they can be heard."

Brocket discovered that his body was shaking and his hands were over his ears until gradually he realized that the sounds he heard were the whines of a baby and the crunch of clinkers under the buggy wheels. He watched the girls pause as Lil lit the lantern. Their faces were white, showing fatigue. Or possibly fear. He could sympathize with that. Nothing would have induced him to enter the tunnel and risk the sight of its ghosts. He waited until the small party had vanished before sliding down the bank and making his way back to his base.

He strode strongly, at a good, swinging pace, glad to be away from the tunnel. No one ventured close to it who knew of its dead.

Was that the reason Mrs. Gimmer had advised the girls to walk down it? To put a stop to anyone following? A person who knew the tunnel's story would shun the place.

Brocket halted. "A patrolman wouldn't do that," he told himself. "He wouldn't be scared because he wouldn't know what he might meet there." That meant that Mrs. Gimmer suspected the person chasing the girls was somebody else.

Someone who kept the dead "in memory." *Someone from these valleys and hills.*

Brocket gasped, shocked at the notion. But there was more to it than that. If Mrs. Gimmer had this suspicion, she must have a particular person in mind.

He went through his reasoning again. There was something about it that wasn't quite right. Mrs. Gimmer was expecting the hunter to give up when he reached the tunnel. Surely after following the girls so far, he wouldn't be put off? Wouldn't he make a detour around the tunnel and, when it ended, continue along the open track? He could be right on their heels.

And Brocket had turned, was running over bridges and stepping-stones, was taking the steep ascent of the slopes at breath-rasping speed, was racing by the side of the tunnel as it burrowed under the hill, was blocking his ears to the groans that whistled drearily from the air shafts, was closing his mind to the sights they conjured while he tried to concentrate on another puzzle, a new question: why should a man who is not a patrolman set out to pursue these homeless girls?

And retching for breath, his head pounding, he at last found the answer. It burst in his head and stayed there, refusing to be dislodged. Appalled, his skin already sticky with sweat, Brocket knew that it was not Ren or Lil that this person was after. It was the baby he sought.

Having emerged from the tunnel, Lil and Ren bumped the baby carriage along the track before reaching another viaduct. Longer than the first, it paced ahead of them on elegant stilts.

"I can't walk much farther," Ren said. She expected some objection, but Lil nodded.

"We'll take a rest soon." Then she saw Brocket. "Just look who's in the rear! Why couldn't he lend a hand with this buggy?" But her tone changed as soon as he reached them and she saw his face. She warned, "Keep up that pace and you'll rupture a lung. Come under one of the arches."

So they squashed together, their backs against the damp masonry of the viaduct, and waited until Brocket had recovered.

He began, "It's like this. I reckon the man after you isn't one of those patrolmen; he lives in these hills. I reckon he knows all about what has happened here, because . . ." and then he halted. He realized that if he continued he would have to mention Mrs. Gimmer and explain that she must have guessed who their pursuer was. He could not do that. He could not bring Mrs. Gimmer into it. Lil would accuse her of some kind of conspiracy. He would not have that said about the woman who had acted as a mother to him, replacing the one he did not even recall.

"What makes you say that?" Lil prompted.

He struggled to circle the difficulty. "Any regular patrolman would have lost you by now, the route you've taken."

"You haven't."

"I live here. How many times have you spotted me?"

She did not answer.

"How many times have you spotted *him?*"

"I haven't counted. Once outside the cave. I didn't get close, but he looked tall. Hefty. Ren thought she saw a head at the roof of the barn. We've heard noises, too: when we were on the lane last night. And there was someone on the viaduct this morning."

"You thought it was me!"

Annoyed by his grin, Lil resolved that he should not hear how she had entered a cottage and foolishly lit a candle.

Brocket argued, "All that's against him being a patrolman. They don't lounge around on a road when their target's a spitting distance away. They don't spy from viaducts. Why hasn't he rounded you up?"

Lil ignored this, pretending to be absorbed in licking the hem of one of her skirts and wiping Found's face. But her fingers were less deft than usual. All day she had puzzled over this question, and it filled her with unease.

"I've seen them," he insisted. "They don't waste time."

"No need to remind me of that." Her voice had altered. It quivered, low.

But Brocket paid no attention to its horror. He repeated, "So why hasn't he arrested you? I'll tell you. Because he isn't a patrolman, that's why. And because he's not interested in you and Ren. He's after that baby. That's what he wants."

They stared at him. They were unable to assimilate his words. Until, her voice cracking, Ren asked, "Why?"

"I don't know."

Finally Lil stated, "You're mad. Just say he isn't a patrolman. What makes you think he's after the baby more than us? What's stopping him from trying to grab her?"

"He's come close. Ren thinks he was on the roof of the barn."

"I screamed for Annie Gimmer."

"That would put him off," Brocket argued. "He's biding his time, waiting till the right moment."

Found had begun to whine and grumble. Lil held her to a shoulder and tapped her back. "Why should some fellow want the bother of a baby?"

It was such a sensible question that Brocket felt foolish. It made his deductions seem ridiculous.

"It's time Found was cleaned up." Lil dismissed his speculations. "I'll use a towel diaper for a change." She removed a bundle from the buggy and lifted up a square of white.

Ren stroked the soft looped fabric. "I haven't seen these before."

"Got them in the cottage. They're the sort babies used to have. You don't throw them away, you wash them."

"Weren't they funny things to leave, Lil?"

"Why?" There was a squeak of plastic and immediately a pungent smell.

"I'm wondering what happened to the baby they belonged to."

Lil shrugged, uninterested.

Puzzled, Ren continued, "If there was a baby, the diapers would go with it, wouldn't they? You wouldn't find any if there was no baby around."

Brocket asked, "What cottage?"

"One in the village."

"They're all empty."

"That shows how much you know," she snapped. "Someone was in it not so long back. It had oatmeal in a pan in the hearth. And candles and matches. And a baby's teething ring, and a battered old doll, and a cup and a box of powdered milk."

"Strikes me that someone's been getting ready to look after a baby."

He could not see the expression on Lil's face, but she was completely still. A sigh came from Ren. Found was quiet, as if waiting for conclusions to be reached.

"I didn't think of that," Lil muttered. She hated to admit

it. She had not questioned whether her plunder had any significance.

"Patrolmen don't store diapers and teething rings and such like in deserted cottages on the off chance they might come across an abandoned baby; but someone living in these valleys might leave the stuff handy when he was planning to make a grab," Brocket insisted.

"I think Brocket's right," Ren was obliged to say, although she didn't like to disagree with Lil.

"And what if he is? What difference does it make?" But Lil knew her question was superfluous. Before this, their adversary had been someone she could understand and she had known what to expect. Now he was inexplicable; he belonged to a region that was foreign to her and was driven by some sinister purpose.

Dejected, she added, "All we can do is keep ahead of him." She searched through her skirts, found a safety pin, and fastened Found's clean diaper.

"If we could get her to Greta . . ." Ren tried.

Lil said, "We can't think of that till we've shaken this fellow off."

"I'll go back and search around," Brocket decided.

"You don't know who to look for."

"I know it's not a patrolman. So I'll look in different places, the crannies they don't know exist." He thought that Mrs. Gimmer would approve.

Lil nodded. "I suppose there's nothing to lose."

"I'll take you where you won't be seen, first," Brocket said and, meeting no objection, he put his hand on the carriage and dragged it over the boggy grass.

NINE

They had not gone far before they saw him. The girls had crouched by a shallow stream while Brocket checked the road they had to cross; then as he led them over it, they saw a figure lift above a slight rise. And although this was the crisis they had imagined, they were unprepared. They halted, their bodies tense.

Brocket whispered, "Let's make a run for it."

Lil's answer was to drag Found out of the sling and thrust her upon Ren. "No chance," she hissed, judging the distance between them, and her hand went for her knife. "We have to make a stand. You guard those two."

The figure drew nearer, waved, and quickened his pace.

"It's no more than a boy," Brocket murmured.

"Hello there!" the person shouted.

"What is he?" Ren gasped.

For the stranger, not much taller than Lil, was festooned with equipment. A rolled-up tent was balanced across his shoulders; a hard hat like a fireman's helmet bobbed at his nape; looped round his neck was a thick rope, and over it dangled a pair of binoculars; maps were slung from his waist. Underneath all that, his clothing was neat, with no tear or blemish, and his boots were of strong leather polished a gleaming brown.

"Where are you heading?" he asked Brocket. Then he saw Ren behind him and the baby in her arms. His mouth gaping, he caught sight of the knife point at the base of Lil's fist and sprang back. His eyes swept over them as he calculated whether he had room to escape. Then he took a deep breath, assumed an expression suitable for combat, slipped his binoculars over his head, and swung them from the strap. "Who's first? You?" he addressed Lil. "Or can you only fight in threes?"

"We don't want a fight," Ren said.

"Depends," Lil qualified, then challenged the boy with: "Do you live near here?"

He shook his head. "I've only been here four days. No, five, if you count the day I arrived."

Impatient with this scrupulous answer, Lil demanded, "So how come you can just . . ." She nodded toward his equipment and to the wide country around them. "Just walk about?"

"Why shouldn't I?"

"You're not an absconder, then?"

"Of course not."

"Then I reckon you're working for the patrolmen," she concluded, a menace in her voice.

The boy's astonishment almost equalled that on seeing the baby. "I don't work for anyone. I'm on my own."

"Doing what?"

"Studying this region."

His answer was so preposterous, so out of tune with their danger and flight, so free of terrors, that they were speechless. At last Brocket's laugh expressed their relief. The others joined him and Found spun out a skein of bubbles.

The boy blushed. "Now that I've given you a laugh, I'll say good-bye."

Before Ren could offer the apology she intended, Brocket asked, "What're you studying it for?"

"What *for?*" The question disconcerted him.

"I've been studying it for years." Brocket considered it necessary not to be outclassed.

"It's not only the geology I'm interested in," the boy confided as to another enthusiast. "It's the evidence of habitations as well, as far back as I can find."

"I can tell you about them."

"I'd appreciate it if you would. Also, there's a henge I'm looking for." He began to unfold a map.

"We haven't time for prattle about habitations; we've got our own to find," Lil interrupted.

"A henge is more of a site, sort of religious," he corrected diligently.

"Is it? Have you seen anyone?"

The boy frowned. "I think I have. Now where was I? Do you want the map reference?"

"I hope you aren't being sarcastic."

"Why should I be?" He was totally mystified. "Don't you carry a map?"

"Oh, forget it! Who did you see?"

"The person I met? I've no idea. It was a woman."

"Annie Gimmer? Was she really old?" Brocket asked.

"She didn't give her name, and I couldn't possibly guess her age. She asked if I'd seen a young girl in a green jacket." He peered for colors under the dirt and addressed Ren. "I suppose she meant you."

"Someone looking for me! It could be Madge." She felt dizzy; her arms seemed as if they would snap under Found's weight. Disobeying Madge's order, she had left the cave and rescue had passed by.

Brocket and Lil said nothing; each was working out the significance of this missed opportunity.

The stranger regarded them, puzzled. "I'm afraid she didn't mention where you could find her. At least, I don't remember. We talked for a while about other things."

"What things?"

"There are quite a number besides making appointments to meet," he answered Lil tartly. "Goats, for a start. Sheep, too, and what happens at lambing."

Again they stared at him, incredulous. Lil said, "Sounds nice. It's a pity we haven't time to hear about them. We need to get off this road."

He nodded and bent his head over the map. "I've no time to spare, either."

("I could've throttled him," Lil said when they were back on their path. "All he was interested in was his rotten old map.")

Feeling her glare, the stranger looked up and regarded her for a moment; and then his eyes rested on Found. Bored and fretful, she was struggling as Lil lifted her back in the sling. "I'd say what you need at the moment is a little coup," he commented. "They were used to drag cattle feed over rough ground and had runners like sleighs. I've seen diagrams."

Brocket laughed and gestured toward their buggy and packs. "You can lend us a tractor and trailer if you've got a spare."

"Come on," Lil urged. "If you meet a fellow asking questions, you haven't seen us. And we haven't got this baby. Understand?"

"Not really. But so far I've met only that woman."

"Well, remember—you'd be sorry if you squealed." Then they left him, forcing the buggy over the stones and bracken, but Ren ran back and whispered, "If you see her again, that woman who was looking for me, or another one called Greta, please tell her you've seen me. She's promised to come and get me. I'm Ren, and they are Brocket and Lil. What's your name?"

"Hilary. Won't she need to know your route?" However, Ren had already gone.

Resuming his walk, he said to himself, One issues threats while the other asks a favor. Added to which, all of them are roaming about without a map. Dad would have been dumbfounded. The height of folly he would have called it. "It's essential to have everything planned," he would say: "equipment, food, route, down to the last detail. I'll take you up to that region, give you a good grounding, start you off. It won't be long before I'm well enough to go back." But he never was.

"I liked him," Brocket said, unconsciously fueling Lil's irritation.

"Who was he? Looking for some 'henge'!"

"I would've liked his tent and some of that rope," Brocket murmured.

"He's all style and no innards. There's no mud on his boots."

"He keeps them polished, that's why. Next time I go down to the service station, I'm going to look whether there's any like them waiting to be pinched."

"Just sauntering about! Not a care," Lil went on.

Her grumbles continued, but Brocket did not interrupt them. He saw no reason why the boy should be interested in their problems; indeed, he was relieved that he had not asked about them. Brocket was tired of questions. What interested him was the boy's business. Or pastime. He did not know which it was. But to walk these hills with a purpose was intriguing; it might even be exciting to do this studying, as the boy called it, to use maps, compare what you found with the illustrations in books. He had seen one or two of those in abandoned cottages, but he had been disappointed to find few contained pictures and was put off by their moldy smell.

"I wouldn't mind giving that a try," he told Ren.

"What?"

"Roving about with ropes hanging off you, and a sound tent—not a rickety one in tatters—and with leather boots on, and having it all tidy in your mind."

"Why?"

"It'd be something to do." His enthusiasm was dampened by her listlessness. Then at last he understood the reason for it and for her pinched face.

"That Madge won't have given up, Ren." He wanted to prevent the tears from swilling down.

"I don't suppose she'll keep on looking. Or the person she sends." Sliding a hand into a pocket, Ren sieved the stones through her fingers. There were four. "They can't do it forever."

"Of course they'll keep looking. They'll not go back till they've found you."

"If they find us, so can the hunter."

"There's something in that," he admitted. "Only your person'll be in the open, not like him, so we'll see her. And Mrs. Gimmer's got eyes in her head like a hawk. She'll see her and pass the word," he said encouragingly, and was gratified by Ren's smile.

Walking ahead of them, he dragged the carriage through gaps between blocks of rock, not high but paving the ground as far as Ren could see. White-streaked and deeply fissured, they were bald of vegetation until they narrowed to form a long causeway and were scattered with trees. These were misshapen, angular, almost bare for the winter months.

"We aren't stopping here," Brocket told them. "Those ash trees don't offer any shelter. Farther up there's a shippon." He saw that they were puzzled. "A shippon's a place where they used to keep cows in the winter. On these uplands, even cattle couldn't take the frost!"

"I could've done without the tree sprouting out of the roof," Lil said when they reached it, but added, "I bet that smart aleck on the road couldn't find this on his map." She smiled at Brocket to suggest he should receive her remark as a compliment.

Inside, they stood and shivered. No longer warmed by the walking, they were chilled by the whistling drafts.

"Mother forgot to pack my gloves," Ren said.

Two days earlier, Lil would have mocked her for being so dependent on her mother. Instead she promised, "We'll find something."

"We're in for a frost," Brocket warned. "But you can't chance a fire. The smoke'd be seen across the whole valley. I'm going, use the daylight that's left."

"Won't you be hungry?" Ren asked.

"I've got some oat cakes from Mrs. Gimmer. I thought I could try laying a false trail. I'd want a few things of hers." He nodded toward Found.

Lil took out her knife, examined the buggy, and pried off a length of plastic trim; Ren spooned the last measure of powdered milk into Found's bottle and handed Brocket the empty box.

"I'll not go far wrong with these," he said.

They were standing in one half of the building, in the open chamber where the tree grew and rabbit holes pocked the soft floor. On the other side of a partition built to waist height was the second part of the shippon, where the cows had been kept. Stalls had been made for them with low walls of boards. Brocket caught Ren's eye and stabbed a thumb toward one of them.

As she joined him, he announced loudly to suggest he was showing her over the premises, "They milked the cows in these stalls." Then, in whispers: "Look, Mrs. Gimmer gave this to me years ago." He fumbled under his sweater and drew a thong of leather over his head. On it was threaded a small hoop. "Farmers used to hang them up in the shippons, so as no harm would come."

"What is it?"

"A witch stone. It's for scaring them off. The hole has to be bored by water, Mrs. Gimmer says."

She held it in her palm and examined the tiny, perfectly rounded window sunk in its center. "I hadn't thought about witches." She did not confess that at first she had imagined Annie Gimmer was one.

"Best to be on the safe side."

The stone was smooth, a milk color tinged with rose; in the half light of the cow stall it shone a faint satin from rubbing against his chest. Ren thought she had never seen anything so lovely.

"Won't you need it?"

"You take it. There's Found, too, and someone, something, we don't know what, is after her."

So she looped the thong round her neck and felt the stone slide under her sweater, unexpectedly warm against her skin.

When Brocket had gone, Ren confessed, "I don't like this cow place. I wish it was smaller. I wish the door at the end of the stalls hadn't fallen off. We can be seen."

"No different from the barn," Lil reminded her, "but I can tell you, staying put gives me the jitters." She did not believe that their pursuer could be defeated by the tunnel; she could not persuade herself that Brocket's strategy of leaving a false trail would work. "The other one can catch up."

"We mustn't go till Brocket comes back," Ren pleaded, and was only partially satisfied by Lil's answer: "We'll take stock tomorrow."

They raked over the floor and fed the baby. Using some orange juice from the store in the buggy, they washed her bottom and changed her; they dressed her in a clean suit and another jacket against the increasing cold. When they had finished attending to her, Lil said, "Your turn now," and cut holes in a pair of socks to improvise mittens.

However, occupation busied their hands only. It could not distract their thoughts. Making a neat row of the cans, both noticed how short it was. Then, dressing Found, they both saw that she was dirty, that the folds of her throat were sticky with food, and that she was patched with a rash. But they did not comment on any of these things. Nor, when their tasks were ended and it was growing dark, did they give words to their sense of an imminent threat.

They arranged their sleeping bags in the larger chamber and lay down with Found between them. They watched the night enter the stalls, but they did not express their fear. They did not admit that they were in readiness, but neither had removed her shoes.

Their good-nights were: "There isn't much wind; we shall hear" and "I'm all ears" and "So am I."

Thus they listened, but they did not know for whom.

TEN

They didn't have to wait long. Ren closed her eyes in order to listen more comfortably and dozed off. When she woke up she thought that it was morning before she realized that the chamber was lit by the moon. It splashed into the broken roof and through the tree's branches, which made filigree shadows on the bright floor. She heard Lil whisper, "There's something. I'm going outside. Stay with Found. Take this." Ren's hand was lifted and her fingers were pressed round the handle of a knife.

Ren knelt over Found, the blood thundering in her ears, Lil's knife clutched in her palm.

"I've done a complete circuit and turned up nothing," Lil reported. "I must have heard that tree scraping against a tile. But on the hill across from us, there's a light. I have to climb up to it, to check."

"Shall we all go?" Ren wished she could control her voice; it was always tight and thin when she was frightened.

"One's better for scouting around. There's no danger here. If it'd make you feel better, keep the knife."

Ren made a gruff noise, and was not sure whether it was to mean refusal or acceptance.

Lil was zipping up her body warmer, pulling on gloves. "It's a lot colder, really sharp. Be back soon."

There was a pad of footsteps and the crunch of dried twigs. That was all. The tiny sounds rippled the silence; then it settled again, heavy and ominous in the vast depths of the night.

At least I can see; the moon never came into the cave, Ren argued, trying to be bold. Then she realized that, sitting in the dazzle of light, she herself could be seen as clearly as if it were day. Immediately, her fingers crippled with panic, she tore off Found's blankets and crawled with her into the shadow at the base of the tree. Half-roused, the baby coughed and began a confused whimpering, and for a moment this and Ren's soothing breaths were the night's only sounds. Then gradually she thought she heard others, heard the darkness spawning small creaks of wood, pinpoint clinks of metal, brief crackles of stiff fabric. She held her breath, her mind begging the noises to cease. They did so momentarily, then were replaced by scratching against planks, the suck of a mass heaved up, the slither of boots somewhere among the cow stalls, then the thud of them on the wide chamber's floor. They hesitated at the edge of the light's shaft; and, her jaws clamped against screams, Ren felt the darkness expand, shudder, split open, and disgorge in horrible slow motion first the boots, then trousers, layers of jacket, muffler, waterproof cape, and finally a cap pulled around a face that showed spectral under the white moon. Talon fingers came up and shaded the eyes; they peered into Ren's corner. "I can see you. You've no reason to hide," the voice cajoled.

It belonged to a woman.

Ren did not move. Clutched to her, the baby's body pressed Brocket's gift hard against her chest. "I've got something that turns away witches." Her breath wheezed.

The mouth was drawn open again; a tongue could be seen between broken teeth. "I'm no witch. I shan't hurt you."

"Why have you come?"

It seemed the mouth's slit had been a smile. "Only to see how you're doing. You've walked a good distance. I've brought you milk and apples."

"We don't need them."

"You will." A bag was dropped onto the tangle of blankets. "You should feed the baby the milk. Lest it grow sickly."

As if in agreement, Found began to cry.

"I don't like to hear that. A baby should be happy. It shouldn't be left to wail," the woman scolded.

"She's not being left. She's scared. You frightened us."

"She does a lot of screaming, too. What do you do to her?"

Indignant, Ren defended herself, "We don't do anything. She has to exercise her lungs. Lil says all babies do it."

"They may where you come from. What do they care about babies? Whip them, shove them into factories, push them down the mines."

"I don't know what you're talking about. Nobody does that."

"They do as bad. What's the difference between them things and casting them out to fend for themselves on the streets, or handing them in to an SCU?" She heard Ren's breath jump and hiss away drily. "Well, I suppose that's better than dumping them, small as they come, by the road," she conceded, with an impatient sympathy. "Let's have a look at this one, see if she's as healthy as you make out."

Ren gripped the child closer.

The woman's voice rose. "Let's see. Where're your manners? Didn't your mother teach you respect?"

So, obedient, Ren held Found up to the visitor's scrutiny.

"You're not afraid of me, are you?" the woman addressed Found and put out a hand. Stiff fingers tapped against her cheek. Found stopped her noise and stared. "There you are," the woman crowed at her success. "I found young Brocket. Has he told you?"

"No." She would think about that later. At present she felt uncomfortable about the woman's hand crooked at the baby's back.

"Annie Gimmer was there at the time, but I saw him first."

"You know Mrs. Gimmer?"

"We walked the drove ways together when we were girls. She wouldn't let me have him. She said I'd taken to wandering too far."

She leaned over the child. Shadows of the hawthorn's branches raked backward and forward across her face; they left small flues of darkness in her eyes, her nostrils, behind the points of teeth. "She needs a proper mother to see to her. Why don't you let her sleep? You put her down and cover her up."

The voice was gentle. Ren heard neither deceit nor threat. She knelt and laid Found on a sleeping bag in the sparkling moonlight. "When she cries, Lil knows what to do. She'll be back soon."

"I'd forgotten that," the woman murmured.

For a sliver of time the shippon was silent. Found lay in a nest of blankets, warm and secure. Then the woman swiveled her head, checked Ren's position, bent down. Two hands sliced through the web of shadows, broke into the moonlight, and the baby was swinging up, up through the band of brightness and into the thick dark. There was a second of incredulous quiet. Then Ren was scrambling over the sleeping bags, shouting, "Leave her alone," and the woman was shouldering her aside. "Give her back," Ren shouted again, and she was jostling her, trying to snatch, while the surprise of her retaliation pushed the woman into a stall.

"Keep away," a voice thundered. Boards cracked, broke apart, and somehow Ren, too, was through them. Splinters tore a hand, but in the other was something hard and sharp. Now there was no breath for shouting; lungs fueled only pants and grunts. In the darkness Ren was clutching, tearing at clothes, clawing for flesh. The woman, with Found screaming against her breast, was straddling another partition, and a foot lashed at Ren's face. But the swing missed its target and Ren had her hands clamped round the ankle, was dragged after it, winched by powerful muscles over more planks, and tossed up. Thrashing like a hooked fish, she hung on to the foot, her opponent hampered by Found and unable to use her hands. Until, attempting to tighten her grip, Ren discovered she was hindered by the thing she held in her palm. Without pausing, she gripped the handle firmly against the heel of her thumb and, piercing first the coarse fabric of trousers, the layers of flannel and underpants, she plunged the blade deep into the woman's leg.

She heard the squeal tear through the shippon; it lanced

the rafters and scraped along the stone walls; it deafened Found's screams. Ren heard it long after the foot jerked out of her hand and the boot kicked her chin. The sound of it still rang in her ears as, stretched across the shippon's threshold, she lost consciousness, her hair stiffening as the dew froze on the flagstones. But that was after she had seen the woman crawl, raise herself painfully, hoist Found to her shoulder, and limp slowly away.

When she had left the shippon, Lil had moved quickly over the scant grass toward the belt of trees they had passed that morning. Beyond it, the light flashed. But at the trees she was stopped by a wall of rock. Impatient at the delay, she peered for handhold crevices, scabs of lichen and minute pits in the vertical face. She was thankful for the moonlight. Without it, she would not have escaped injury when she reached the top. For she had to stride over bottomless cracks between the huge blocks, their surface slippery, scooped into hollows by rain.

Once over this hazard, she saw that the distance from the light was greater than she had thought. It was on the opposite side of a valley, and she had to descend the hill, cross a railroad track and a road. Then she came to a wide stream. Running beside it, Lil looked for shallow water, a place to cross, but within a few minutes she had reached a footbridge, was over it and running, her breath jangling and chest tight. Climbing hillocks and mounds that reared tall as mountains, she saw as she grew closer that the light was set high and that within its misty aura it seemed to move.

Was this a signal? And if so, to whom?

Lil resisted the question; otherwise her legs might have stopped without her bidding; they might have turned and carried her back to the shippon that she had left in Ren's trembling guard. She could not allow that. She had been taught to complete a mission; you did not retreat from your goal.

And suddenly she had reached it. She balanced on rubble that had once been a hearth, looked over the stump of a chimney, and there was the light. It came from a lantern fixed to a tall pole and shone out undimmed by the moon. Hanging from straps, it was sufficiently loose to swing in the breeze. No one was occupied in sending signals. No one was poised to attack her.

Lil stood in the ruins of the cottage and her body sagged with relief. She would have liked to rest, but she had to wait until she was back in the shippon, lying in her quilted bag, cocooned against this cold. She could not remember when she last had a full night's sleep. "It's not clever to push yourself beyond your strength," she had been told many times. "Afterward, there can be penalties. You may be less efficient and take foolish risks."

Thinking of this warning, she looked along the slopes and to the horizon as far as she could see. Above her the lantern fluttered. She wondered whether telegraph wires had once been strung across this valley and whether this pole was all that remained. It was certainly tall enough. "You would need some muscles to shinny up that!" she said aloud, admiring it. "And who did? What was the point of sticking a lantern on the top of a rotten old post?"

The night was quiet, waiting for her to understand the question. Then she was shouting the answer: "It has a point!

It's been strung up there on purpose. It's bait. For me. To lure me away."

Again she was running, away from the light now, racing down the hillside, tripping over tussocks and into stiff clumps of reeds. And while she groaned at the trick that had been played on her, one part of her mind was warning her that this was not the way she had come. The river she had crossed had been too wide to leap. What lay before her was a stream she could straddle, and its water was little deeper than that covering the marsh. Looking at the land around her, Lil realized she was lost.

She did not know how long she wandered. Time did not tick at an even pace; it battered and hammered, its strokes always coming more and more quickly. She hacked through deep bracken, alarmed that she could not see what it covered; she slopped through slime, fearful of what congealed horrors might lie under its skin; she found watercourses that seeped up through the peat; and she followed their slim threads only to find that they sank again into the earth. She had nothing to comfort her. With her legs dragging and her face growing numb in the night frost, Lil thought of Ren and Found left undefended and again remembered her people's training.

So she trudged, hopeless, her meandering way lit by the leering moon. When she crossed the rails and found the great blocks of stone, she was not sure that they were the ones she had climbed earlier. When she saw the shippon, she imagined it was a mirage, a destination beyond her reach.

But it remained in her quivering vision, a flimsy fortress with a gaping doorway and a hawthorn tree flapping through its roof. Running toward it, she heard her throat issue strange, scraping whimpers that became sobs as her boots squeaked on the flagstones, as she caught sight of a blade filmed with brown, saw clothes, arms skewed across the threshold, and the bruise patching Ren's face.

ELEVEN

It was Lil's hands rubbing hers that brought Ren back to full consciousness. She could not move. Grief clamped her muscles. Not before her stiff body had been heaved, dragged, and placed under blankets and her hands pushed inside the sock mittens was Ren able to speak.

"I couldn't stop it."

"You tried," Lil's voice consoled.

"The stone would have worked if there'd been a witch."

"Stone? You had my knife. Remember? There's a lot of blood. You must have jabbed him hard."

"Her."

There was a pause. "You mean, a woman?"

"She was tall; and so strong."

"You're sure it wasn't a man?"

"Her voice." Until she had started screeching; then she was like a wild beast.

"Can you remember any more?"

"She said . . . she found Brocket when he was a baby."

"Brocket? Was he left, too?"

"Mrs. Gimmer wouldn't let her have him."

"So now she's taken Found? I've got to find her. No, you can't come," she stated as Ren tried to rise. "You've been knocked out and you're as stiff as a corpse. Keep under the blankets. When Brocket gets back, say he's to make a fire. The time's past for trying to hide."

"Where will you look?"

"Where the footprints go. She's made a mistake, stealing Found on a night when there's frost."

It was some time later that Ren, huddled by Brocket's bright fire, recalled how Lil had pushed herself clumsily to her feet, the floor's litter furring her damp knees and exhaustion bleaching her face.

"I'll follow her soon as I can," Brocket had promised. "First thing is to get you warm, or else you'll take sick."

"I don't care if I do. Please leave me and go after Lil. She'll need help. We have to get Found back. Please, Brocket."

But she could not persuade him however much she begged. He had nodded and continued to collect kindling for the fire, splitting planks, climbing the shelf above the stalls, throwing down brittle twigs, pulpy wood, and handfuls of moldy hay.

"I've told you, I'm going. I'll be off soon. I'll find them, Ren."

He could not tell her how glad he had been to find

her. There had been the scuffed prints in the doorway, the splintered wood in the stalls, and finally the tangled bedding. It had taken him several moments to accept that it did not cover Lil or the baby; and examining the bruise on Ren's face, touching her icy cheeks, he had thought she was dead. He wanted to forget the feel of her cold skin under his touch. Then she had moved, breaking his nightmare, and he had told himself, I must warm her up.

When the fire was burning, he tugged her to it, draped her with sleeping bags and blankets. At last, ready to go, he asked, "What happened?" Aghast, he listened, and watched her tears licked by the light of the flames.

"It's not your fault," he told her, and knew that was no comfort.

"I shouldn't have laid Found down. Just because she told me to. I should've kept hold of the baby."

"She'd have gotten her all the same. She's bigger than you. It would've taken someone her own size." He did not add: None of us is that.

"Annie Gimmer didn't let her."

Brocket thought: Mrs. Gimmer has never been in charge of the baby. Ren's feverish. She must be raving. "Mrs. Gimmer would see to it that Found wasn't grabbed," he soothed.

"Not Found. You." Now that tears had begun, there was no time for words.

"Me? Mrs. Gimmer hadn't let her grab *me*? When? Who?"

She shook her head. Her body was lifted, jolted by sobs.

Appalled, he said, "It don't matter."

Through great retches she managed, "She travels. Farther than Annie Gimmer."

Brocket considered. There was a memory. It eluded him, a will-o'-the-wisp. He caught a glint of its passage. It led him to the buttress of a lime kiln long abandoned by farmers. Moss furred its curved stones, primroses dotted its entrance; there was a haze of bluebells somewhere by trees, and Annie Gimmer was saying, "You stay here; try splicing those ropes I've brought; and don't you make a single sound till I get back."

Mrs. Gimmer had been hiding him! "I never saw anyone," he murmured. There had been times when he had been shooed away from the shed or barn or shippon that Annie was using.

"She said she found you. Mrs. Gimmer wouldn't let her keep you."

Once he had sneaked back and, unseen by Annie Gimmer, he had peeped in. The place had held nothing of interest, only a mound of old rugs and sacks out of which came a hoarse cawing and stentorian snores.

"Don't cry any more, Ren," he pleaded, thinking: I need a weapon. Looking around for a piece of timber or a stick that could be used as a bludgeon, he remembered metal glinting near the doorstep. He went out, found it, and his fingers closed over the haft. There was a crust of brown on the blade, and he shuddered. But he must not be squeamish. Ren had used it.

Returning, he told her, "I'm taking Lil's knife," and dropped it into a pocket. However, before he had whispered a farewell, there were noises: a slithering, the bump of a body lurching against wood, the scrape of feet dragged through the floor's loose earth. Then there was a fat roll carried in the crook of an arm, a sleeve glistening, and a figure leaning into the light of the fire.

It was a second before they recognized that the person was Lil. Her clothes were sodden; her skirts clung to her legs in drenched swaths; under them, her trousers wrapped sopping bands over her flooded boots. Little remained of her cape except a tattered fragment that collared her neck, and down her body warmer ran a wide slick of green slime. Dripping strands of hair snaked over her shoulders, then were threaded by sharp grains of frost.

But it was her face that had caused Ren and Brocket to imagine that they were looking at a stranger. It was unlike any face either of them had seen. It was polished with sweat and streaked with soil. Blood from her split nose trailed over her lips and down her chin. Long welts curved along her jaw and came together in bruised knots at her throat.

"Lil," was all Ren could manage.

She turned in Ren's direction and her eyes glided over the other's swollen, blotched face, but it seemed that she did not see it, or anything of the girl who had spoken. She merely responded to the voice and stood, regarding the space it had come from.

"Lil," Ren repeated.

She flinched, and for a moment strove to understand her surroundings, but her eyes remained unfocused and her expression continued blank.

"Shall I take the baby?" Brocket asked her.

Lil started. She drew the bundle back, gripped it against her shoulder.

"You're wringing wet, Lil. Let Ren have Found and I'll help you dry yourself."

They waited as Lil, her face immobile, worried at the sounds until gradually she absorbed their meaning. She looked around, found Ren, and knelt at her side. But it was some time before she would relinquish the bundle. She pulled the covers from the child's head, removed the sodden bonnet, massaged the cold nape, and stroked the damp cheeks. She smoothed the blanket on Ren's lap, laid the child upon it, and arranged Ren's arms. Then she stayed by Ren's knee.

Brocket asked, "What happened, Lil?"

As his hand tapped her shoulder, she jerked away and swung around, an arm thrown up to protect her face.

"It's me, Lil. Brocket. Tell us."

Her silence was terrible.

"You are with us now, Lil. Safe."

The word made a crack in her abstraction. Her cheeks twitched.

"And so is Found. You've brought her back."

She nodded. Laboriously, her lips worked. "Yes. Not taken again."

"We're glad, Lil. Has the woman gone?"

She tilted her head, as if listening to a distant sound. "Gone, now." She slid away on her knees, leaving damp tracks over the floor. Passing out of the firelight, she reached the corner and squatted under the tree.

Ren screwed up the edge of a blanket and dried the baby's face. Found looked back at her, white and frightening in her stillness. "Is she all right?" Ren appealed.

Delaying the answer, Brocket said, "We'll take these things off her first." They removed stiff oilskin and a strange, checkered shawl and unwound strips of cloth.

"She hasn't taken any hurt," he pronounced, stating their relief. "She's dry under all this." Clasping a hand, he was pleased that the baby resisted; it was another good sign. He put more wood on the fire. "Better get her warmed up." He adjusted the blankets and sleeping bags into a tent for them both. The baby was crying now, but fitfully.

"She's hungry," he diagnosed. It seemed to be the main

complaint of babies. They could be kidnapped, brought back, messed with, and the only thing they could think of was the next meal. "That's why she's making those whines."

To Ren, they were moans. "She's tired out," she said. "I'll lie down with her in a minute. What about Lil?"

He wished that Ren had not prompted him. He had been planning to collect more sticks, boil some milk for the baby—there was a full can on the floor. He had even thought of gnawing at an apple, for he had found a heap of them near the milk. He would have grabbed any excuse not to approach Lil.

Her face terrified him. The glazed eyes looked inward, were fixed on something else, some demon or horror that had penetrated the bone and taken up residence. A living, mocking presence inside the skull.

Despite this, Brocket forced himself to go to her, to say: "You have to get out of those clothes, Lil; otherwise you'll catch a fever."

She did not answer or raise her head; therefore, he knelt down and, hesitantly, expecting a repulse, he pulled her feet toward him, untied the saturated laces of her boots, and dragged them off. Lil took no part in this; she did not kick, or assist with the fused knots. But when he had torn off what remained of her cape and said, "Your body warmer, too," she swung away from his hands and put her own over the zipper.

He was tempted to leave her. His thought said to him, Let her take sick, die if she wants; see if I care. But his feet did not move him away from her, and his fingers taught hers to grasp the zipper's tag and ease it down. After that, there were sweaters and skirts and the great, sucking tug of the trousers. At each garment, Brocket had to coax, arrange

Lil's hands, guide them, lift. He continued until her arms were bare and her shoulders, tawny in the firelight, showed above a grubby vest.

Only once had he seen anyone naked, when years before he had bathed with Annie Gimmer in a pool below a foaming fall, and he had felt neither curious nor shy; but now he suddenly knew that Lil wanted privacy. He turned and reached for a covering. Still silent, she allowed him to drape it over her and did not squirm as, using a diaper, he rubbed at her hair. Then somehow he maneuvered her to where the others were sleeping, slid her into her bag, and laid his on top. Her expression did not alter, but he was relieved to see her lids flicker and close.

It was not until he had built up the fire and wrung out the wet clothes that Brocket admitted his own weariness. When he had decided to help these girls, he had not imagined he would end up being a nurse. Mopping up. Either tears or river water. Brocket groaned to himself.

The moon had vanished, but the sky had not yet signaled the new day. He hoped that dawn would somehow be delayed, granting him a few hours' sleep. After this night, he could hardly remember the previous day, but he knew that it had begun with Mrs. Gimmer. She had told him, "Those girls have cleared out. Take this lantern and say they're to take themselves through the tunnel." He had carried out her orders—done more. However, he had seen no sign of their hunter and the false trail he had set had been no use. The man after them was far too clever. Brocket corrected: Not a man; a woman. Who had wanted to keep him! He would ask Mrs. Gimmer about it. Because memories were floating in. He saw himself sitting on a road, looking at the tire marks of a truck in the grit; and he had remained there—for how long?—until fingers had forced a straw full of milk through his lips and a figure had wavered, vanished, reappeared in his misted sight.

He zipped up his jacket, placed his knapsack as a pillow, and lay down. Shuffling his haunches, he felt the prick of a point: Lil's knife. His hand moved to his pocket, then stopped. He would keep the knife. Out of harm's way. Lil was always flourishing it, and as soon as Ren had it, she stabbed a person twice her size in the leg. He had often imagined a companion, but nothing like these two.

Reflecting, talking to himself, Brocket remembered a bruised, sobbing face, a shoulder bare and ridged with bone, as were his. More distant, there was harsh panting, the voices of two women, a spiral of dust, and himself being lifted, stuffed into a pouch of clothing, and carried off. Until at last these pictures clouded and Brocket slept.

Thus in the last hours of that night Brocket joined Ren and Found in a sleep that was solid and dreamless. None of them was woken by the other beside them. The strange moans and screeches that came from Lil went unheard.

TWELVE

Throughout the next day, Lil neither moved nor opened her eyes. The only sound that came from her was the breathing that sawed in her throat.

"Don't you think we ought to wake her?" Ren asked.

"Mrs. Gimmer says there's not many cares sleep doesn't settle."

"How did she get so wet?"

"There's the river."

"But that's miles away. We walked by the side of it before coming to the viaduct."

"Not that one, another, in this valley."

Long before Ren was awake, Brocket had been up to examine the tracks outside the shippon. He had been surprised by their number; they radiated in every direction, but he dared not investigate them. He could not risk leaving the girls alone when the woman might reappear. Already he had made a mistake: he had taken no precautions against her the previous night. Waking with that knowledge, immediately making sure that Found was still with them, he had felt the sweat blooming on his skin. The negligence was inexcusable; he was thankful to have been granted such luck.

"Do you think she swam across?" Ren could not imagine it.

"Down there, it's not much more than a stream. In places you can wade through it. And there are footbridges."

"I suppose she could've slipped in." Gently Ren traced a finger down the spine of Lil's torn nose.

That and the drenched clothing were all they discussed. They made no reference to the welts on Lil's throat. Neither invited the other to deduce what had caused them. They wanted to keep their minds away from frightening speculations; and they chose not to talk about whether the woman might return.

Ren merely nodded when Brocket placed a large stick by a tin and told her: "While I'm out, bang that if you've need. I'm fetching water. I won't be long."

Gradually, however, as the morning passed and no one appeared, they began to feel safer.

They laid the baby on her stomach in a patch Brocket had smoothed clean. A low fence of planks he built round her protected her from drafts and, propped on a wad of clothing, she was able to stretch her arms and dabble her fingers in the stalky dust. Occasionally Ren went to her and worked her legs.

"What's that for?"

"Lil does it. She's teaching Found to crawl."

"I hope she masters it soon, then. Instead of us carrying her, she can just trot behind."

"Oh, Brocket!" Ren answered, and saw him grin.

After that, more cheerful, they collected fuel for the fire, tearing wood out of the stalls and climbing to the loft for dried bracken and hay. They hung Lil's clothes over packs to make sure they dried thoroughly. Agreeing that she might become too hot, they dragged her in her sleeping bag to a cooler place. Ren tackled Found's diaper.

"It's not so tight as when Lil does it," she criticized.

"It's a neat job." Brocket approved. "Changing a diaper isn't such a bother when you know how."

"You can do it next time, then," Ren told him, and smiled at his alarm.

After that, they fed her, both of them nervous and neither pretending to have superior skill.

"She's letting the purée run down her chin, Brocket, and she hasn't eaten as much as usual. Look, she turns her head from the spoon."

"Maybe she's tired of it. Or she's taken a chill."

They dressed her in extra clothing and placed her nearer the fire. "Not too close," Ren warned, "or she'll get blisters." Therefore, they tested the heat on their own skins and discussed distance.

When it came to a meal for themselves, they enjoyed the novelty of food heated over the embers, but they decided they should open only one can. Counting them, they had been worried that so few were left. "I'll have to fetch some when Lil's woken up," Brocket said.

"We'll all go."

"We don't all have to trek back."

"Where to?"

"The cave."

She heard his fear. "If we rationed ourselves, perhaps we could get to that freight depot Lil talks about."

"It's a good hike."

"I'll have to do it one day, if Madge doesn't find me first."

And then what about me? he asked himself. Easy to answer that: When I'm rid of this bunch, I'll do exactly as I did before.

But he could hardly remember what that was, and he suddenly realized how much he enjoyed the company of Lil and Ren. Although Lil always wanted to rule the roost, she was brave and tough; and Ren had her own kind of courage. He was accustomed to the usual sorts of danger such as chasms and precipices, flash floods, goblins and ghosts, but danger with these girls had more point. It occurred to him that he was responsible for it. If he had not left Found with Ren, she and Lil would not have been chased.

"You'd reach there faster without the baby. I'll take her over, if you want," he offered.

"I've made her a promise." She stroked the baby's soft cap of hair.

"Mrs. Gimmer'd help. She'd see that other one didn't get her. Found would be better off brought up in these hills." Babies soon grow up, he told himself. Then he could show her about—all the best places.

"It's nice where Greta lives. It's not all computers. Perhaps she would know how I could bring Found to show you."

Brocket nodded, consoling himself with, The special places will keep.

Absorbed in their thoughts, they were startled by a call at the doorway, and before either of them could rise, someone entered the shippon and strode between the stalls.

"Good afternoon," Hilary greeted them, and for a second they could only gape.

He had arrived so suddenly, and once again his appearance so contrasted with their own, that he seemed to have stepped from another world. His clothes retained their polished elegance, his complexion its health, and his eyes were neither bloodshot, as theirs were, nor ringed with the dark stains of fatigue.

"I trust I'm not intruding," he responded to their stares. "This shippon looked like a good place to snatch a rest. But it's lucky you are here, because I can tell you . . ." About to step over Lil's bag, he saw that she lay in it, and was arrested by the marks on her sleeping face.

"We've been in some trouble," Brocket told him.

Hilary nodded, apparently not curious, but looking at Ren, he permitted himself a raised eyebrow at her bruise.

"It wasn't them fighting each other." Brocket thought it was necessary to make that clear.

"I'm pleased to hear it. I was thinking I should keep my distance," and they all laughed.

"She needs something to put on those wounds," Hilary said, nodding at Lil and unbuckling his pack. Unlike theirs, it smelled of soap and polish and was divided into compartments, all labeled. "My filing cabinet," he observed. "Later, of course, the notes will be transferred to disk."

Astonished, they watched him don eyeglasses and study the labels on the knapsack's contents. "Here we are: emergency medication. Cream for boils, no. Burns, no. Constipation?" He looked around, received no bids, and returned to his search. "Chilblains, no? Diarrhea, no. Emetics—I inherited all this from my father. Gnat bites? Not in this weather. Impetigo, ugh! Lacerations. This is more like it. Lacerations, lesions, and minor wounds. This stuff might be worth smearing on that," he addressed Ren's chin; "but it seems more appropriate for those," he prescribed for Lil's welts.

"But you may want it," Ren said as he handed the tube to her.

"If I do, I can find something else."

She nodded. It seemed unlikely that he would lack for anything when he possessed so much.

Brocket asked, "What did you want to tell us?"

"I've come across a cart. I'm afraid it's not the sled kind with runners but the usual sort, with wheels. If you're interested, I can tell you where to find it."

"Thanks. It might be worth a try. We have to move on again soon."

"Not immediately, I hope. I predict another frost."

"I wish we could stay where it's warm," Ren murmured.

"You should. That baby's looking sick."

"I expect she's hungry. She didn't eat all of her last meal," Ren told him, and tried to soothe the child's whines.

"It might not be a good idea to take her out."

Brocket agreed, but: "We're running short of food. We've hardly any left. Trouble is, we're miles from any I know how to lay my hands on."

"There's some in a valley southeast of here."

"Where? I've never heard of it."

"Do you know any of the old lead mines?"

"Yes. Which?" Then Brocket added quickly as Hilary pulled out a map, "Just give me the landmarks."

The other chanted them off as a finger climbed effortlessly up the hills, colored brown on the paper, leaped down the vertical cliffs of limestone, and glided along the blue ribbons of rivers and streams.

Brocket thanked him. "I don't know of anything nearer. I think we'll have a look for it, lift a few cans."

"You're welcome to take what you wish."

Until now, they had not understood that it was his own food Hilary had offered them. "I don't like to take yours." Brocket would have been happier to steal from a cache owned by someone anonymous.

"There's plenty. The only drawback with the frozen stuff is, if you're hungry, you have to wait till it's thawed."

"You mean you have electricity!" Ren exclaimed before Brocket had worked that out.

"I just rig up what I need."

Brocket thought, Rigging up his own electricity! Mrs. Gimmer would be astonished.

"Is it far?" Ren asked.

"Quite a distance, and it will take you longer with the baby." Found was crying, wriggling and swinging her head. Hilary watched as Ren took her up, rocked her, and patted her back. "I tell you what: if it would help, I think I could spare the time to get you the cart." He took out a notebook and examined the entries. "Yes. I'm a little ahead of schedule. It's west-northwest of here. I could be back with it some time tomorrow. Save you the trip," he told Brocket. He rose.

"It's getting late," Ren said. "Why don't you sleep here?"

Hilary hesitated. "I must say you've made it very cozy."

At the center of the chamber, the burning wood crackled, shifted, and the flames raced upward, never still.

"It's quite a temptation," he admitted, but it was one he could resist. He heaved his equipment onto his shoulders.

Watching him, Brocket thought, He doesn't want to get too mixed up with us. I don't blame him!

"Oh, there's something else." Hilary leaned against a

wooden pillar, in no hurry now that his going was settled. "About that woman who was searching for Ren—I remember her name: Cob." He saw them exchange glances. "I've kept a lookout, but I'm sorry—she's been nowhere near my itinerary."

"Where was that?"

"West. Were you expecting her?"

Brocket flinched. "Sort of."

Hilary said, "I suppose she could still turn up. Funny name, Cob."

When he had gone, Ren said, dejected, "So it wasn't Madge or Greta that was looking for me."

"One of them, someone, will turn up," Brocket encouraged her. "I'd lay a bet on it if I had the cash."

"It was that Cob looking for me." She shivered. "And she's the one who took Found. Is she really gone, Brocket?"

"I can't pretend with you, Ren. We just can't be certain whether she's gone for good or not." They were admitting the fear both had suppressed all day.

"We'll have to take turns to be guard."

"Won't you be frightened, Ren?"

"Not as much as before. You and Lil are here."

"I'll take the first shift. I'm not very sleepy," he lied.

"Should we put more wood on?" Ren asked.

"I think we might as well keep the fire going."

Ren slid into her sleeping bag. "I've still got your witch stone, Brocket," she told him as she felt it settle hard on her chest.

"You keep it."

She thanked him. "I like it so much, but if you've always carried it . . ."

"I have, only now Hilary's given me a compass."

"I don't always understand what he's saying, but he's nice."

The shippon was warm and still. Only the creaks of Found's breathing and Lil's snores interrupted its peace. Beyond the ragged firelight, the doorway was invisible; the cow stalls did not exist. Outside, the mountain was silent.

Ren's anxieties were lulled by the quiet and the soft flames. Her eyes were closing. Tomorrow Hilary would bring the cart; they would pull Found in it; they would reach a cache of food. It would be a change to eat enough. And she did not have to struggle to keep awake now. Brocket was keeping watch.

THIRTEEN

It was not Found's crying or Brocket's summons to do her shift that roused Ren the following morning, but Lil's voice: "I've been stretched out twenty-four hours. You should've woke me."

Still curled in a dream of her mother smiling, showing her a newborn child, Ren could not respond.

"You needed a rest," she heard Brocket say. "And it worked."

"I've got to clear out."

Ren was aware of the ripple of flames. They gilded the baby laid on another's knee and cast nervous, agitated patterns onto a young woman's face. It was not her mother's; it belonged to Lil.

She managed to ask her, "Does your face hurt?"

The other ignored the question and dipped the corner of

a rag into a can of warm water, disturbing its faint plume of steam. "I wish I could give Found a proper bath. She's a mess, all foul and runny. I bet she caught something off that woman."

"Why do you say that?" Brocket asked.

"She stank. When I've finished, I'm going."

"We have to wait for Hilary." They told her about his visit and his offer to bring the cart. "He says he'll be back by afternoon."

"That's not soon enough."

"Half a day won't make much difference to the food," he objected.

"Food?"

"We're almost cleaned out. I told you. Hilary's lending us some from the stock at his base and we're going for that, soon as he brings the cart."

"I'm not waiting."

Irritated, he demanded, "Why're you set on running off so quick?"

"It's none of your business."

"Well, *thank you.* I didn't bring you that lantern. I didn't show you the paths. I didn't lead you to this shippon. It wasn't *me* that made sure you had shelter." He halted. He did not like to mention that he had also put her to bed. The reminder would embarrass them both.

"And I suppose it wasn't you who came across the baby the first night." She turned to Ren. "I was never told that. You said you'd found her outside the cave. I never did think much of the lie."

Ren blushed. Even if Brocket had not been present, she could not have admitted to Lil that she'd wanted to keep him to herself.

The other girl sniggered as if she guessed.

She arranged Found's legs astride her knee, took her hands like reins, and trotted her up and down, but it was clear that the baby did not enjoy it. Her head swayed, and she gave thin, fretful cries.

"Is there anything wrong with her?" Ren asked.

"She's probably cutting a new tooth," Lil diagnosed, and lifted Found up to her shoulder.

"Since Ren didn't let on, who told you it was me who brought the baby?" Brocket demanded.

"Leave me alone, will you?" She was up, Found clutched in her arms. "I got her back, didn't I? Whatever that old hag said, I've cared for her as well as anyone could. Better. Her idea was to bind her like a mummy in strips of mucky cloth and run off with her into the bitter frost. It's a wonder she's still here after what she's gone through."

He did not flinch. "What has she gone through?"

"I got her back. That's all that matters. I got her back. No one else did. So now it's up to me to decide. And I'm not hanging around, waiting. She's coming with me." Ren began to climb out of her sleeping bag.

Brocket said, "You can't just walk off with her. She isn't yours."

"She isn't yours, either. You passed her on."

"I'm not saying she's mine." He was almost shouting. "I don't own her." What did he own? Nothing except a broken penknife and a threadbare sleeping bag.

Lil did not answer. She was pushing Found's hands into mittens.

"It's like she's a lump of meat," Brocket protested. "First one person grabs her and rushes off and then another."

"That won't happen again. You're safe with me now," Lil

spoke to Found. She stroked the newly wiped head against her cheek. There the welts were thick and prominent, their color a dark crimson. At Lil's throat, where they met, there was a web of scratches and flaps of torn skin.

Ren said, "Hilary left this ointment. It says on the label: 'Apply twice daily.'"

Lil refused the tube. She was gathering her outer garments, thrusting an arm through the body warmer while clinging to Found. "If you're coming, get packed," she ordered Ren. "If you aren't ready soon, I'll start."

Brocket was dismayed to see Ren's hurried obedience. He asked, "Are you expecting that woman to come here again?" While she pondered his question, he thought, I'd get more sense out of Mrs. Gimmer's goat. "Are you?"

Eventually Lil answered, "I got rid of her."

"So, what's wrong with hanging on here for a bit?"

"Stop going on at me, will you?" One-handed, she was cramming clean diapers into her knapsack, along with baby food and matches. "I've had enough of this place. I can't stand it. That great hill." She pointed where, beyond the walls of the shippon, the ground pitched gradually toward the mountain. "All those rocks!" Her voice was shrill. "I can't bear it. I feel hemmed in."

"Hemmed in? *Here?*" Brocket laughed, but he followed her to the doorway. "Which way will you go, Lil?"

Her gaze swung across the slopes and up the massive hill, and her lips worked. "Not along there." Where her eyes pointed, there had been tracks, but he had been unable to read them, transparent smears in the dissolving frost.

Scratched by her fear, Brocket shivered. "There's a road at the bottom. I'll fetch the buggy." He realized that he spoke to her as if she were ill.

He joined Ren, who was packing their belongings, tossed the remaining cans into a bag, scooped dust onto the fire, and stamped on the embers until their glow shriveled and they collapsed into gray flakes of ash. Then, as a sign for Hilary, he laid a line of twigs on the floor, adding bent ones for arrowheads and pointing them toward the road.

They had all benefited from the day's rest and, taking a path downward, they covered the ground quickly. Even so, it was not fast enough for Lil. She would race ahead of them for twenty yards or so, then stop and upbraid them. "Can't you do better than stroll?"

"We'll show you how we can stroll if you aren't careful, and see if you like it," Brocket told her.

After that she made do with clicking her fingers and chewing a strap she had rammed between her teeth.

They soon reached the tracks and, a little beyond that, the road. "Did you cross this the night before last, by any chance?" Brocket asked, pretending innocence, but it was wasted on Lil. She simply turned south and hurried on.

The road was in better repair than the others they had traveled; therefore, Ren and Brocket found pushing the buggy easier. But they could not catch up with Lil. Despite the weight of the baby, she was almost running. From time to time she would glance over her shoulder and look toward the slopes they had left.

"Do you think she's afraid there might be a patrolman?" Ren asked. She was alarmed that they were ignoring this particular threat. "We shouldn't stay on the road."

"There's no more cover off it. Besides, I reckon the patrols will be pulling out. They're delicate, run at the first hint of frost. And look, on the top there's been snow." Streaks of white draped down from the long, flat crest of the mountain. "That'll finish them."

She had to trust him. "You ought to tell Lil."

"More likely she's scared that old Cob woman'll turn up."

"But she said she got rid of Cob."

"For how long? When she's rested and tended to the leg, she might come back."

"What will we do? What if she tries to grab Found again?"

"She got the worst of it with Lil, so she'll not take on three."

"Can't we catch up with Lil so that we'd be nearer to Found if Cob jumped out?"

"Don't be such a worrier, Ren. I'd get there. I'm fast on my feet. Show you sometime."

When they had walked a little farther, Brocket added, "Lil didn't say it was Cob she had to get clear of. Remember? It was the *place.*" He shivered. "I know how she feels. There's plenty in these parts that's best left alone."

At last Lil's pace slackened. Reaching a bridge, she halted, and with her back turned to the land they had passed, she looked across the slopes and contemplated the peak that lay ahead.

When they caught up to her, she greeted them with, "Do you know a path around that?"

Brocket said, "Yes; nobody ever tried building a road over it."

This mountain lay like a sleeping creature, its blunt head massive, its spine groomed with snow.

"But me and Ren don't mind if you want to climb up and give us a wave."

Lil tutted. "So we go on along this road, then?"

"Not before I've had a bite to eat. I'm sick of this rush.

So Ren and me are having breakfast. We've pushed it long enough."

"Let's go another mile or two," Lil negotiated, and they trudged on.

They stopped under trees by the side of the road and shuffled through grass crisp with frost. Above them, branches rattled their last leaves.

"I'll just try Found with a drink," Lil announced. "She refused her food this morning." She drew the baby from the sling, and they all examined her. Found twisted restlessly, and her lips screwed.

"She looks pasty," Ren said. "Perhaps it's the traveling."

"I can think of better seasons for it," Brocket commented. He dredged through brittle undergrowth, dug out the rotting trunk of a tree to serve as a bench, and selected a can for their meal. "But it can't be helped. Morning or afternoon, with or without the cart, we have to get to Hilary's supplies."

"I'm not bothered about the food," Lil muttered.

"We've guessed that." However, Brocket did not question her again and Lil was grateful.

It was only when they had eaten and were walking up a track, and that harrowing moor was finally behind her, that Lil could speak of the terrible night.

FOURTEEN

"When I left the shippon, I didn't know where to look," she told them. "There was a mess of footprints in the frost, so I thought it would be easy, but it wasn't. The prints went everywhere, some around and around the shippon as if the old woman had circled it, over and over again. Like someone crazed."

"More likely she couldn't make up her mind to go in," Brocket suggested. "When you're old, you're plagued with second thoughts, Mrs. Gimmer says."

"She was crazy, I tell you. She'd set her mind on getting this baby. Whatever the cost." For some minutes Lil said no more, her head slanted away from them, concealing her expression.

"I followed one set of tracks a good distance before I understood that they were my own. I'd made them coming back to the shippon only ten minutes before, and they were pointing the wrong way! I was going for anything, without properly examining it! I was acting like an amateur, getting sloppy."

They were incredulous at this confession. Brocket thought, It's nice to hear her criticizing herself for a change; while Ren consoled: "You were tired out, Lil. You'd been up all night."

"Not then. It wasn't over.

"I was glad there was a moon. It helped me pull myself together, and I found that the line of one set of prints was uneven and the mark of the left boot slithered. She was limping, wounded in the left leg. You did a good job there, Ren. So at last I had found the right tracks.

"I didn't know what start she had on me but I reckoned that, lame in one leg and carrying a baby, she wouldn't go fast. I misjudged her. She could move as swiftly as anyone I know.

"At first the footprints weren't difficult to follow. She was traveling more or less on groundlevel, keeping to the contours of the hillside because of the injured leg. That was a relief. I'd had enough climbing for one night."

Lil paused. There had been strange, unintelligible craters; the prints would lead her toward one, then veer round its lip, and her steps would be threatened by hollows that were flooded with darkness. She dared not dwell upon what they might harbor or how deep their base might be. She remembered Brocket had told her that this region was pitted with holes, deep shafts that led into passages under the earth, tunneled by springs. If she were to trip into one of them, she could not be saved. She would lie torn and smashed while subterranean waters swirled over her. A solitary corpse.

"What is it, Lil?" she heard Ren ask.

"A memory," she answered, and stifled the moans. As if in sympathy, the baby whined drily. Lil pulled her closer.

She went on: "At some point the footprints stopped. We had hit water. Not a river or a stream; I wished it had been. They have banks. This was the sort that spreads all over, oozing out of the ground. There were prints at the start, in the mud; then they disappeared and I didn't know which direction to take. My boots were already sodden, so it was no shock when the water came over the tops. But it slowed me down and seemed to be sucking me in and I was thinking, What'll happen if I can't get out? I couldn't see far. The moon was still there, but it couldn't show where this water ended, or if it went on and on, or if it got deeper. And the picture of Found kept coming to me, of her being dropped in this mucky stuff and lying there and sinking till it rose up her head and swilled over her face and filled her nose and mouth and all that was left of her was bubbles."

"Oh, Lil! No!"

"Yes. By the time I caught up with that woman, I was about as crazy as her.

"I was still splashing, looking for Found instead of signs of the woman, when I had a slice of luck. It was the only one I had in the whole night. I felt a breeze. It caught more than me; it found something else and I saw it stir. It wasn't Found, though. The thing was a length of rag. It had been ripped off a skirt and it was soaked in blood. Two strides away from it, there was grass again, and a heap of stones. She had bled on those, too. It came over me that, for the first time in my life, I was the hunter. I would've been sorry for almost anyone in that condition, injured, burdened, in piercing frost, but I couldn't pity her.

"The splashes of blood went on, over low tables of rock, so following her was no problem. Up to then, I hadn't seen her. It's amazing; the slopes are so barren and from a distance seem to offer no cover. But when you're on them you find that there are dips and spurs that cut off your view. You can be close to someone without knowing it. And I was.

"I reached a narrow channel. Soon it became a stream. Then suddenly there was an open space. I was in it before I saw her, not more than six paces from me, crouched over the water, scooping it in her palm and sloshing it on the injured leg. By her side was a bundle. She hadn't heard me; her moans were too loud. All I needed to do was to leap forward and grab.

"But I didn't do it. I just stood there, trying to get my breath. I couldn't jump when she had her back turned to me. I couldn't come at her from behind. And her leg was sticking out like a crutch, and she was bathing it, bent over as if praying the water to put it right.

"Then she must have sensed I was behind her. She swung around, saw me, slid to where Found was lying, put herself between us, and snarled like a cornered dog.

"If Found hadn't been at stake, I would've run off. She was wearing a cap and its brim was bent, jutting up sharp as a beak. Under it, her skin was like ashes except for her nose, which was purple, rawed by the cold. In the moonlight there were black, empty sockets where her eyes should have been; but it shone on her teeth. They had points like fangs, sharpened to spike you and rip you open.

"She growled, 'So you've come chasing.'

"'I'm here for Found.'

"'You're not getting her.'

"'Give her back.'

"'This isn't a game.' She reached down and picked Found up.

"It was too late to go for her: she was holding the baby. I couldn't risk it, and I said to myself, You've got to find some way to fool her. Only, there was nothing I could think of. She had more cunning than me. She'd already proved that by luring me away with that light. I tried to recall what I'd been taught, but nothing fit. I just stood there and she watched.

"'The baby'll soon be hungry,' I told her.

"'Don't you try telling me how to care for her. You can't even dress her properly. She needs swaddling clothes. I saw to them first thing.'

"'We've kept her in clean diapers.'

"'Not if it hadn't been for me. You filched those I'd saved over the years in readiness.'

"That told me that the old-fashioned diapers had been left by this hag. It must have been her head Ren saw at the roof of the barn. I can't work out why she didn't take Found that night."

Brocket suggested, "She was so close to where Mrs. Gimmer was resting, she had to be careful. She wouldn't want to risk Mrs. Gimmer interrupting when she was snatching Found."

Lil nodded and went on. "She yelled, 'You can go your way. You've got a few screws loose if you think I'm handing her over. She's not yours. I found her. Up a path top of the valley, not far from the big road. I was bringing her along the old cattle way. She would've stayed with me if that young Brocket hadn't interfered. If he hadn't stumbled on the carriage. I'd left it with the wee creature tidy and slumbering inside it while I climbed down past the cave to the brook. I had such a thirst on me with pushing the carriage. I should've gone back the moment I heard him roaming, but I stayed on his heels for a bit, see what he was about.'"

"It was her stalking me! Not Yordas," Brocket exclaimed.

"What?"

"No matter."

Lil continued, "Then she said, 'By the time I'd been to the brook and climbed back, that young Brocket had nosed out the carriage. And he took off with her. Sheer mischief, it was. He didn't know what to do with a baby. He had to pass her on to you.'

"'He didn't pass the baby on to me,' I told her. I was stalling, trying to keep her talking while I worked out a plan. 'It was Ren he gave her to.'

"'Wren! More a young vixen at bay with her pup.'

"'You frightened her.'

"'Not enough. She stuck me like I was a pig.'

"Her teeth mashed like pincers in front of her tongue, which was rolling round in her mouth, and I was thinking: Ren wounded this ogre and I can't get anywhere near her. But my legs were buckling under me; they had covered miles over punishing ground.

"She'd pushed her leg out as if to show me, and I said, 'That needs another dressing,' and she nodded and began to croon over Found. She said to her: 'I'll borrow a length of your swaddling bands, flower bud. You'll not grudge me that?' She folded back the waterproof and unzipped her, and I could see Found was wrapped round with strips of cloth, squeezed tight as in a straightjacket, but she was asleep. She even looked comfortable. The old harridan began to unwind a piece of the cloth, talking all the time to Found. I thought, She'll have to put Found aside in order to bind the leg.

That'll give me a chance. First, I'll jump at her and give a massive clout to the wound; secondly, while she's rolling in pain I'll sink a rabbit punch on her neck; and thirdly, I'll grab Found and race off."

Lil halted her story.

Ren said to herself, So that's how she rescued Found.

While Brocket, more astute and not underestimating the old woman's toughness, thought, That way, Lil wouldn't have kept the baby for long.

Looking at her, they found it hard to believe this was the same girl who had confronted them earlier: strident, willful, claiming a right to the baby. Now her face was intense, shocked; nerves plucked in the cheeks and stitched down the ridges of welts.

Brocket prompted, "She was unwinding some of the swaddling bands she'd put on Found."

"To make a bandage for her leg," Ren added.

"Yes."

They waited for her to continue. But suddenly there were shouts and in the distance behind them they saw a figure pulling a cart. Hilary. There was no time then to coax Lil to tell them the rest of what had happened.

Later in the day, Brocket took Ren aside and whispered, "Lil didn't get Found back the way she had planned. Up to then, she hadn't been in enough water to get so soaked. It's made me wonder if . . ."

Ren caught his shivers. "I can't forget the wounds on her face. It's as if they were made by claws."

FIFTEEN

It was Lil's injuries that Hilary first commented upon. "I hope you had a good rest," he addressed her after his greeting. "You needed one, having sustained such wounds."

His words pierced her abstraction, but all she could manage was, "Yes."

"How are they feeling?"

"They sting." She was charmed by his interest.

"Your bruise is looking paler," he remarked to Ren.

She nodded. She and Brocket were examining the cart Hilary had brought. It was small, boxed in at the sides, and balanced on two wheels.

"This'll be a help," Brocket commented.

"I found some oil and greased the axle." Hilary pulled the shafts, demonstrating the smooth movement of the wheels.

"Pity a horse doesn't come with it. You must have strong arms!"

"I've always kept in training. One of my father's principles."

"Does he do research in these valleys, too?" Ren asked.

"He is dead."

The tone was matter-of-fact, but Hilary turned his eyes away and none of them could think of anything to say to him. As they stood gathered round the cart, suddenly each wished for someone else to be there with them. Each longed for warmth and shelter and older shoulders upon which could be hung their troubles. For a few moments this trek was too long for their hunger, for their tired feet and splitting boots.

Then Brocket said, "It's getting colder." His words became delicate feathers of steam. "We must go on."

They lifted the buggy into the cart but left Found in the sling, deciding it was wiser not to disturb her until her next feeding. To Ren's offer to carry her, Lil answered, surprisingly, "I could do with a rest. But she'd wake if we swapped her over. It's taken her long enough to go to sleep."

That was true. The baby had grumbled and whined during most of their tramp that morning. But she had not disturbed their listening, her noise had so matched the story Lil told.

"I'm going your way until this road nears the lake," Hilary told them. "I want to have a look. It's interesting."

"Why's that?" Brocket asked.

So Hilary began a discourse on thawing glaciers as they threw their packs into the cart and each took a shaft.

They made a strange caravan: the cart pulled by the two boys, one so smart and polished, the other sooty with smoke, his clothing filthy and shapeless; Ren, white and scrawny, her sneakers gaping, a sleeve of her parka slit open, streaked with an old woman's blood; Lil, her skirts frayed, the tatters of hems fluttering around her ankles, her face swollen and bruised with eyes that stared as through slits in a mask. And lastly, inside the improvised pouch and swinging to the rhythm of Lil's walking, was the baby, zipped into a quilted suit, snugged by a woolen bonnet, who made neither a movement nor a sound.

Therefore it was not her demands but their fatigue that finally brought them to a halt.

"I'm starving," Brocket said, panting. The others were pleased that someone else had admitted it, but they could see no shelter where they could eat. Hilary scrutinized the land through his binoculars, then handed them around.

"See, in the angle of those two walls, that wire and what looks like chopped-up wood?" he pointed out. "I think there's something behind them."

So they left the road and pulled the cart up a path still hard after the night's frost. Reaching a heap of posts and the coils of rusted wire, they discovered behind them a shelter.

"I wouldn't have guessed that without the binoculars," Brocket said admiringly.

Ren asked, "What is it?"

"An old horse trailer."

It stood by the stone wall, out of the wind. Its wooden panels were warped; one of the doors had vanished, but the roof remained sound. Having only two wheels, half-sunk into the ground, it rested at a slight tilt. They crawled in and lay down.

"Hay! Best thing in the bed line," Brocket murmured, his eyes closed.

Lil said, "I don't like to be reminded of horses."

"Why not?" Ren asked.

"Security uses them. When they're after you down narrow places where they can't get the vans."

They were quiet, their thoughts quivering.

Brocket, distressed by the scenes he imagined, went to unpack the buggy and select food.

"Only three cans left," he reported.

Lil groaned. "It's bad marching on an empty stomach, my great-great-grandpa always said."

"You don't have to open anything yet. I've got some stuff. Sorry. I'd forgotten." Unfastening his knapsack, Hilary pulled out packages of oatcakes and chunks of crisp meat.

"Rabbit!" Brocket exclaimed.

They divided the meat among them but left half the oatcakes until later. Hilary declined his share of those. "I've already had a couple. When the old woman handed them to me, she urged me to sample them."

"You've seen her again?" Their eating stopped. Their faces turned toward the open end of the trailer. Their eyes scanned the limitless moorland, searching for the figure Lil had described.

"Not the one I met before," Hilary explained.

"Who, then?"

"I didn't enquire."

"Mrs. Gimmer," Brocket decided. "It's her way with meat."

"She certainly knew you. When she heard I'd be seeing you again, she asked me to give you this food. She wasn't looking for you. She was searching for the other one."

"Who?"

"That other old woman I told you about—Cob."

Lil swung to Brocket. "What does that mean?"

"Mrs. Gimmer suspects it's Cob who's after Found. She'll be trying to stop her."

Lil dropped her head; her eyes were on her fingers picking at her skirt. "I wish Mrs. Gimmer'd come sooner," she muttered.

Brocket told Hilary, "It's Cob that kicked Ren on the chin the night she kidnapped Found. Lil brought the baby back."

Hilary blinked. "Do you mind repeating that?"

So they told him everything. And although their story frightened them again in the telling, it lifted their spirits in an unexpected way. For it reminded them of what they had accomplished and how they had endured. Hilary was included. Listening, he became one of them.

"It's odd that I didn't notice anyone prowling around," he commented, and was surprised by their smiles.

He was thinking about the welts framing Lil's cheeks. The story had not explained them. Hilary reflected, to himself, They must have been made in a desperate fight, and none of them wants to describe it, so I won't ask.

Later, alone with him, Brocket said, "I could see you were mystified about Lil's wounds. So are Ren and me."

Therefore Hilary was pleased that he had been tactful and asked no questions. He took a handful of hay, buffed up his boots, and said, "Well, I suppose I should be moving on."

"It's time Found was fed." Lil lifted the baby out of the sling.

"She's had a good sleep," Ren remarked. "It's a shame to wake her up." Then, alarmed, she asked, "Is anything the matter?"

The baby's eyes were staring unfocused into the dim light of the horse trailer and didn't respond to the faces gathered around her. And when she was held above Lil's knees, Found didn't stretch her feet but flopped against Lil's chest, her whole body limp.

"Is it a tooth?" Ren stroked a cheek, white, no longer firm. "Why doesn't she cry?"

"Give us one of your deafening yells; it'll do you good, Found," Brocket urged. He was speaking for them all. Noise would have been a relief. The baby's silence was unbearable.

They knelt around her, examining her, hoping to catch her attention, trying not to compare her with some inert, voiceless doll.

"Snap your fingers in her face."

"What for?"

"See if she blinks."

"What'd that tell us?"

Finally Hilary suggested, "We could try taking her pulse." No one made a move so, overcoming qualms, he reached for a hand. It did not respond to his touch; the fingers did not circle his. Tiny, they lay on his palm, spread like soft petals, the nails translucent shells. He took the wrist, held it delicately between finger and thumb. "It's going like mad," he informed them, and with his eyes on his watch he counted the blood beats. "But I've no idea what it should be at her age."

Lil recalled, "My mother says babies need plenty of liquid when they're teething. Perhaps she's only thirsty."

Ren said quickly, "I'll put some water in her bottle."

They could not tempt her, although each of them tried, and they were afraid she might choke if they pushed the teat into her mouth. All they could do was shake out a few drops and moisten her lips.

"I think this must be more than trouble with cutting a tooth," Hilary offered.

Ren suggested, "Perhaps it's something she caught that night with Cob."

"But if it's a cold, or a fever, wouldn't she be hot?" Brocket asked.

"You'd expect so. Has this come on suddenly?"

Hilary's question made them think back, remember how Found had refused food, how she had vomited a little that morning, how her diaper had stunk, and how she had fidgeted and fretted.

Ren asked, "What about those medicines you've got?"

Immediately there was a bustle, Ren helping Hilary to remove them from his pack, Brocket cleaning a space on the floor, Lil placing the child in the center of it, ready for them to administer pills, syrups, powders, swabs, antiseptics, inhalers, all the remedies for the ailments that Hilary read out. Each time he did so, they chorused their decision quickly, impatient to come to the one that fitted Found. Until, reaching zootoxin ("What's that?" "She hasn't got it.") any hope was finally quenched. They sat in silence around the still baby and regarded her, helpless, appalled.

Eventually Hilary apologized. "You see, my father never expected to provide for a baby."

Lil said, "We'll have to take her into a health-disadvantaged unit."

"There aren't any."

"There are where we came from."

Despite their anxiety, the significance of her suggestion reached them. To save the child, Lil would risk her own future. Their minds could not admit the pictures of her discovery and cruel capture.

"We can't move her again," Brocket argued. "We have to do it the other way around, bring help to her. Mrs. Gimmer is wandering about looking for Cob. I'll fetch her."

"Just a minute." Hilary stopped Brocket, who was already fastening up his parka. "Even if you found her, are we sure she would know what to do?"

"She brought me up."

"Were you ever as ill as this?"

"I don't know."

"I think it's an antibiotic or something we need. I have stuff like that in the old lead mine. The trouble is," he cautioned as their faces brightened, "we mustn't give anything unless we've got the diagnosis right."

"And how do we do that?" Lil demanded. "You're just being petty."

Hurt, he said brusquely, "Better than killing her off. We could find out, if we had the books."

"Books!" Brocket exclaimed.

Lil told him, "My great-great-grandfather had a Bible."

"Sometimes if there was a story I liked, my mother would make a sound-print," Ren said.

"Well, I'm talking about *books*. I know where there are some. It wouldn't take long to flick through and find what is wrong according to the symptoms, then collect what is needed. But the library is boarded up. I'll have to break in."

"Two of us ought to go. I'll come with you." I'll try anything, Ren thought, to make Found better.

"Burglary is my specialty," Lil interrupted.

Finally, after Lil had admitted that her wounds throbbed in the frost, and Ren that she was too tired to keep up the necessary pace, it was agreed that Brocket should accompany Hilary.

They did not delay. "Night's coming on, and there's not much moon," Brocket pointed out.

"It shouldn't be hard to see the pathway south of the lake, though," Hilary reasoned. "It's the route traders and monks took across to the abbey."

"I know, but it's had time to grass over since then."

They laughed in spite of their worry, both relieved to be undertaking something positive and glad to get away.

Ren watched them run down the path to the road. I shouldn't be standing here, she rebuked herself; I ought to be taking my turn in nursing the baby.

But she did not want to do that. She dreaded the thought of picking up the slack body, of feeling it motionless against her own, not wriggling and full of life. She shrank from the sensation of the head lolling against her cheek and of looking down into eyes that regarded her without recognition.

The figures of the boys were small now; they were being sucked into the dusk. She wished she were with them. She envied them the adventure ahead. At home in the living-work unit, she would have been unable to contemplate it. Yet here she was, wishing she could take part in stealing books! Ren sighed, turned to the trailer, and climbed in.

SIXTEEN

Ren did not know how long the boys would be away, and she was glad that neither she nor Lil wore a watch. Adding up the hours she spent nursing the baby would not have shortened each minute; it would not have made the seconds limp past any faster. And on the morning after the boys had left, Ren did not search for a piece of rock to add to her calendar. She no longer wished to record the days and she hid the six pebbles away.

The time went just as slowly when her shift with Found was over and it was her turn to do the tasks. One was to light a fire.

"Is it safe?" she asked Lil, thinking that Cob might still be a threat. "It could be seen—the smoke."

"We need boiled water for Found, so even if there's some

patrols around, we have to take the risk." She seemed to dismiss any danger from Cob.

Therefore, following Lil's instructions, Ren gathered dry gorse and bracken, found the missing door of the trailer behind the stone wall, broke its bowed panels with one of the posts, constructed a wigwam of the split pieces, lit several of their precious matches, persuaded a flame, and at last balanced a can of water on the precarious hearth. Her eyes red in the smoke and her nostrils and lungs repelled by its sour smell, she guarded the vessel diligently. The water boiled without mishap and, soon cool, it was dripped patiently between the baby's lips.

Yet even this occupation, which seemed to go on forever, used up no time at all. Afterward it was still daylight; the sun was fixed in the same place; the appearance of Found had not changed. So Ren did not notice how efficient she was with the fire; nor as she searched for water did she think, A week ago the idea of being alone up here on these moors would have finished me off. All her thoughts were given to the baby; the dread that she might not recover dragged at each hour, and it was a relief when twilight entered their shelter, heralding the night. That was welcome now. Ren could whisper to herself: Hilary and Brocket may be here tomorrow; please don't let Found die before they arrive.

She and Lil did all they could think of. They changed her diaper, wiped her mottled face, and kept her warm. Remembering that she carried a small packet of glucose, Lil rummaged through her knapsack, searched through her skirts, and turned out every pocket. Tracked down, it was dissolved in water and drops were squeezed into Found's mouth.

"Glucose is better than sugar," Lil explained. "It brings back energy."

"It's working!" Ren breathed, as a nerve pulsed in the cheek and the tongue poked and licked. "It's a miracle." But the effect was short-lived. It produced no other movement.

Lil said, "We must be losing our marbles, expecting an instant recovery. We'll keep on giving her this, and we'll have some, too."

"I'm not bothered about energy. I need *food!*"

"This is as good."

"No it isn't. It won't fill me. It won't stop me from feeling that my stomach is swinging inside me like a shriveled-up bag."

"You'll get used to it. We did, when it was dangerous to move."

"My mother used to say, 'Considering your size, Ren, I don't know where you put it all. You could out-eat a horse.' Do you know what I'd like this minute?"

"A nose bag of tasty oats?"

"One of the Festive Foil dinners my mother used to order for a treat. The tray was so wide, it wouldn't slide down the chute for the groceries; the delivery man had to knock on the door. With the meat there was a sauce and red jelly as well as the gravy and vegetables, and real ice cream with the cake."

"I was told that all you eat in the living-work units is dried beef and powdered potatoes."

"I've never seen those on the Fax-a-Feast menu. There was tenderized steak. I liked the Caribbean Barbecue best. It was to go with the leisure-screen pictures of people on a beach. The meat came off in flakes, all crispy, and then there was the bone to suck and, looking at the pictures, you could feel the sun trying to give you a tan." She paused. "What would you like?"

"I'd settle for a stew with dumplings."

"There's a stew for the picture scenes, called Country Idylls."

"They'd get no orders if it went with Street People Kitchens!"

Down to their last can, they rationed themselves to three spoonfuls each meal.

"Help yourself to tomato soup," Lil invited as they crunched the first bean. "No need to hurry. The goulash won't spoil."

"These onions are tasty," Ren told her, and placed another bean on her tongue. "How are the peas?"

"Like heaven! I'm saving the meat chunks till last."

"Don't forget the chocolate bun on the side of your plate."

"That'll do nicely to fill the last hole."

"I feel a lot better now," Ren said, sucking the bean gravy from her fingers, gnawing until the skin was puckered and red.

"There's nothing like a hearty dinner to set you up."

Afterward, they excused themselves, exclaiming, "What a silly game." But they could not prevent it. By the second day, they were thinking about food almost as much as about the baby.

"We mustn't get ill," Ren murmured, "or else . . ." She was kneeling by Found, massaging an unresisting hand between her palms.

"Of course we won't. We've got water. That's all we need."

"I'll go for some more."

Away from the shelter of the trailer, Ren could not dismiss the cold. Inside, dressed in as many layers as Lil, she kept tolerably warm; but outside, her clothes seemed flimsy and insubstantial. They flapped as she walked, and the cold sneaked through. There were no trees, no fences, or even the barrier of derelict buildings to blunt the wind's edge. The faded sun offered no heat. The frost crisped the bracken in her path and stiffened the dew into transparent seeds. When Ren reached the stream, she found icicles ridging the grass; they hung over the flowing water in a ragged fringe. Holding the bottle under and feeling the water's chilly grip on her fingers, she thought, I never knew it could be as cold as this. It never seemed as freezing as this on the leisure-screen when they showed skiing. At least, in the trailer, we can keep Found warm.

She must return to her. Dizzy, anxious, she stumbled away from the stream and onto the bare path.

But it was not empty. There was something ahead of her. It grew larger. Too wretched about the baby to protect herself, Ren shouted, "Please help." She heard herself repeating the appeal as the person came closer, leaned over her, placed one mittened hand on her arm and another under her chin, raised her face, and ordered: "Stop that! Otherwise, you'll get a smack." Then she was pulled into the matted and smelly wool of a coat and her head was held against Annie Gimmer's chest.

"You're an oddity. I never felt such bones," she said gently as she released Ren. "Not looking too good, either. What's all this about?"

"The baby's very ill. We don't know how to get her better." Gabbling, crying, she explained. Then, "Will you come?"

"I'll take a look."

"Hilary met you, didn't he?"

"That's right."

"Did you know the other one, Cob, was after her?"

"I guessed."

"We think she's probably stopped now."

"Yes."

Had Ren been less distracted she might have asked Annie Gimmer how she knew. Instead, she hurried on.

At the trailer, Annie Gimmer leaned against the opening and peered into the shadows. She made no attempt to enter. "Where is she, then?"

Ren announced, "I've brought Mrs. Gimmer, Lil."

"Let's have a look at her. Come on!" Annie Gimmer ordered impatiently. "Hurry up, girl. I'm not after her. I won't lay a finger on her. She's a cursed one, she is, the bother she's brought."

Ren began to say, "She can't help that," but Lil was edging forward. She sat at the end of the trailer, her legs hanging over.

"Show me!"

Obediently Lil turned back the covers and supported the baby's head.

"That's no cold nor fever nor yet a tooth. How come she's like this?"

"She wasn't ill before that old woman Cob snatched her," Ren argued.

"So she got her after all, did she? I had hopes she'd give up at the tunnel. Where was that young scoundrel Brocket?"

"He was laying a false trail. He thought—"

"Children's games!" Annie Gimmer interrupted. "It's about time the lot of you grew up."

"What's wrong with Found?"

"Something to do with her insides, I'd say. Some muck she's eaten. And she's dried out."

"Will she get better?" Ren was not sure that she wanted an answer.

"I'd say it's touch and go." Reading her expression, Annie Gimmer added, "It's something we all have to face. It doesn't run away because we don't want it."

"Can't you do anything?"

"No. It needs medicines."

"Lil's got some glucose. We're giving it to her when we can get it down."

"That might keep her going for a bit, but it's no cure."

Ren defied her: "I'm not going to let her die."

She sighed. "Well, I must say you've got some spirit."

Annie Gimmer's arm, hooked round her pack, trembled. Ren remembered the sound of her boots shuffling through the pebbles; she observed how the skin on her face was pallid, the dirt in the deep wrinkles undisturbed. And Ren understood that when the old woman had talked about the baby, she had not been unfeeling. She herself was sick and old, and she accepted that all life ended.

Desperate, Ren told her, "Found's not going to die. I love her."

"Then I hope you have better luck than me." Her eyes dropped, focused on the girl beside her, and Ren saw that they grieved. Suddenly she wished she were older. Then she would have the words to comfort the old woman, be able to ask who was the friend of Annie Gimmer's that had died.

"I'll be going," the old woman said. "You're welcome to this; you look like you need something solid inside you. I've no use for it now." As she swung her pack inside, Lil raised her head and for the first time showed her face. Arrested,

Annie Gimmer observed sympathetically, "You've been in the wars. Who gave you those slashes?"

She pushed out a hand and, despite Lil's struggles, took hold of her chin and peered at the wounds. She frowned; her back stiffened. Then she took in a great, snorting breath and began to cackle.

"So you carry Cob's marks!" Annie Gimmer exulted. "It's fitting, Cob leaving those prints. She had nothing else." She paused; she became an old woman again, and frail, her brief vigor passed. "But I've got her here," she declared bravely, tapping her head. "Inside."

Then she demanded, "And what did you leave on her? Come on! What?"

The color had left Lil's face. It had drained away so deeply that it seemed no blood was left in the skull. "I don't know."

"I've found the tracks. There were bandages. You were out by the long cave. She led you a dance, didn't she?"

Lil shrank against the split panels. Her eyes were black with the terror of memory.

Ren gabbled, "Lil had to go after her. Cob had snatched the baby from me. It was me that did the wounding."

"Proper little spitfire," Annie Gimmer mocked. "I saw the blood. And whose knife drew it? Yours." She swung back to Lil. "You carried it here, bringing the ways of the street into these hills. Did you use it to butcher Cob, that night under the moon?"

Butcher. The word sliced through the air, scattering the frost.

"No!" Ren stammered. She had to force her tongue to move in her dry mouth. "No! It was left in the barn."

Annie Gimmer nodded, but never for a second did her eyes turn from Lil. "How did you manage it, without a knife?

I know where it happened. I found the lantern. I know where Cob is now. I've seen her cap where it hangs out of reach. Tell me what you did."

The girl's lips worked.

"Tell me, you young demon."

Lil's body rocked. Her throat rattled.

"Cob kidnapped Found," Ren repeated. "She acted like someone mad. It wasn't right to leave Found with her."

"Who're you to say that? You know less than Cob did about babies; and she wouldn't have dumped her like your folks have the habit of."

"But Brocket said . . ." She had to continue the argument; she had to protect Lil. "Brocket said you wanted to stop Cob from having her."

"I did. I tried to catch her, but Cob had the advantage of years and was a prime walker. She knew I was after her and she didn't want me telling her to stop the hunting, to go off, take her sulks into the next valley. But hunted or not, this one here had no reason to do what she did."

To Lil, she shouted, "And what was that? Tell me. You couldn't have done it fair. It must have been a trick."

"Lil fights fairly. She didn't attack before Cob saw her. She couldn't do it when Cob's back was turned." Ren was screaming.

Annie Gimmer was not listening. She repeated, "You couldn't have done it fair. Cob could tramp over this land blindfolded and not come to grief. It must've been a trick. You'd have been taught plenty of those where you were born. And you'd have been taught as well to seek revenge. Well, I have not. Revenge is not why I'm walking these hills, though now I've been brought here, I'm hard put to keep my hands to myself. But I will. And you can tell me how

Cob came to be where she is. It's owed her, the knowing. I might settle her drifting ghost if I could tell her I knew. I can't give her bones burial; I can't shroud her broken relics in cotton grass or the sweet leaves of larch. But she might yet rest decent; she might be appeased if it was known why she lies there. It would be a little comfort in the loneliness if she knew such a memorial was carved in my thoughts."

Her voice had grown thin; her words were prey for the raw gusts. Lil sat rigid, her expression fixed.

The old woman pushed herself away from the trailer. For a long time she remained, swaying a little; a soft keening rippled her chest. "It seems we'll have to make shift without, Cob," she murmured. "But there's one thing certain. You're not stretched in that deep darkness, a pelt full of smashed bones, because you were careless and missed your step. You never lost your skill.

"And I'm sorry now that I forbade you a share in Brocket's fostering. I kept him to myself, believing a wanderer like you, Cob, wasn't right to be for a nurse. But he might have quietened the longing, and your wildness would have passed with the years."

Ren did not watch her going; her eyes were on Lil. She was making strange noises, coarse, grating pants as if she had run beyond the power of her muscles and the stretch of her lungs. Not knowing why the thought came to her, Ren said to herself, I wish she would cry.

Aloud, she told her: "She's gone now, Lil."

The wrenched breathing did not slacken.

"It's over, Lil. She's not coming back. She won't say those things again." She searched for other consolation, but her mind stopped at a body lying in some profound, black pit. There forever. Out of reach of burying hands. She could not ask how it came there. The question stuck in her throat. She repeated, "It's over, Lil."

The skin of Lil's face was taut. Like land under thin snow, the shape of the bones was traced by the low winter light. Still reaching for air, Lil managed, "Over?" Contradicting the word, a shudder commanded her.

"We've got to get back inside. Found has to be kept warm. And we can eat. She's given us food. See." Ren quickly unfastened the straps of Annie's pack. "She said we could have it. She didn't need it herself."

Lil looked at the food Ren held out: more oatcakes and meat. Then her shoulders jerked, her head turned away from the child in her lap as, retching, she vomited. And the watery contents of her stomach fluttered, then trailed like thin whey over the frost-silver grass.

SEVENTEEN

When Annie Gimmer left the trailer, she was in no hurry to reach her goal and walked slowly. But when Hilary and Brocket had set out, they had to reach their destination as fast as they could.

"We don't have to stay on this trail all the way," Brocket said. "Soon there's a shortcut."

However, when they came to the path that curved away from the trail, the night was established and the moonlight was fitful as it wove through the clouds.

"It'd be risky with the moon bobbing around," Brocket judged.

"Then this is the moment to camp. I didn't notice this path on the map. You'll have to show me tomorrow."

"I can find it."

"I know, but I have to see on the map where I am and where I've been. Otherwise how could I find it again?"

Hilary repeated his request the next morning. "Is this where we are now?" He tapped his map. "Past the position marked 'water sinks'?"

"That's behind us, just off the road."

"So we go along this path as far as the gorge. Then what?"

"We cross where it's narrow."

"But a bridge isn't shown on the map."

Brocket laughed. "There wasn't ever much call for one. There's a way down. You'll see."

Hilary felt sick at the prospect. Trying to find an excuse to avoid the route Brocket proposed, he argued, "There could be ice."

That was true, for the frost had struck again in the raw hours before dawn, sliding under the bracken they had laid over their sleeping bags, needling through the quilted fabric, pricking into clothes until it found the warm skin. "It might be better to keep to the trail." Hilary said.

"That's farther. This way saves time."

Hilary said no more. He folded up the map, ate his share of oatcakes, strapped his sleeping bag to his knapsack, and followed Brocket along the path. But his heart drummed as they approached the gorge, and when he stood at its edge, it was as bad as he feared.

"It's pretty steep," he remarked, trying to sound nonchalant about a drop that looked vertical. He hoped that Brocket would assume it was the exertion of walking that caused his erratic breaths. "We'd better find somewhere to fix this." He fingered the rope he carried.

"No need. All we have to worry about is loose stones."

Brocket began to climb down. Hilary adjusted his pack and went after him. There was nothing else he could do.

The first few yards were unremarkable. The path went down rocks that formed rough, irregular steps, and there were shrubs, which provided twigs and branches to hold on to. Boulders also were a help. Great wedges of tumbled rock, they were often his height, and he could drag his hands along them, lean into their stable bulk as he circled them. But rounding one, he found nothing. He was standing in the air. His boots might be resting on a path (a path you did not wish to see the angle of, yet all the same, a path) but he, Hilary, was hanging there unsupported. His stomach whirled.

A voice addressed him. It was close but faceless. It said, "Hold on to that sapling and and use it to swing to where the rock juts out."

The condition of Hilary's stomach was affecting other parts of his body; he had to force his hands to be still before he could latch them around the slender trunk. Using it as a tether, he slid around; but to reach the rock, he had to release his grasp of the sapling and plunge. In that second of time before the rock hit his groin, his skin spouted sweat. He heard, "Take it slowly! And watch out for the loose stones."

Hilary could not see them. On his right, the cliff face rose up, a mass without limit; on his left, the ground dropped away. He was on a natural shelf running diagonally downward. It was no wider than the soles of his boots. His hands groped, found crevices that provided holds for his fingers. Thus he shuffled sideways, his back turned to the void. Then his finger-holds ended. The opposite side of the gorge was close, erect and massive. There was a jet of foam.

"It's lucky there's been no rain; this waterfall's thin as spit," Brocket shouted up.

Hilary took no notice, for the surface under him had shifted and he was slithering, sliding downward on stones that rattled and tumbled under his boots. He felt as if he were hurtling into a funnel.

"That was clever," Brocket greeted. "I allus come down on my backside."

Hilary did not hear the other's congratulation. His head rang as he saw where they stood.

They were in a narrow trough where the walls of the gorge almost met. High above them the rock rose straight up, and despite the faraway patch of sky, the place was enclosed, dark and threatening. Hilary put his hands on a boulder in front of him and tried to recall his father's explanation of such places, but all he knew was the weakness in his legs and the pain in his stomach, which had begun to pitch again.

"Nearly there," Brocket told him.

Hilary understood then that they had not yet reached the bottom of the chasm. He saw a heap of boulders, another fall of water.

"You go down alongside this spout. It's no more slippery than usual," Brocket said.

Hilary looked at the rocks, at the water as it dropped to its final bed, and although that was only fifteen or twenty feet down, he could not move forward. "I think I'll climb back."

"You dropped something?"

"No."

"What, then?"

"I won't be long. I'll find another way."

"What're you talking about?"

"I'll meet you on the other side."

"You can't do that. You'll be hours. What's wrong with this?"

"I'm telling you, I can't go down there."

"Be careful and you'll get away without even wetting your boots!"

"It isn't the water. It's the height." He had said it, and he heard the echo of his voice, shrill and childish, against the frowning rocks.

"But this is nothing! Look where you've come from."

"I don't dare." He wished he had fallen, had plummeted into this pit. He wished he now lay shattered upon the great spikes of rock, his blood trailing over these boulders to foam brown in the fall of this stream.

"It's easy to lose your nerve," Brocket told him. "Turn round, crouch down, and grip that piece that's sticking out, then bring your legs back. I'll guide your feet and tell you when to drop your weight. You can keep your eyes closed, if you like."

After that, Hilary could not argue. He had to carry on. Like a child he lay on the topmost boulder, let his feet dangle, and waited until Brocket had caught them and pushed them into a crack. Then he released his clutching fingers and slid downward while Brocket held on to his waist. He did not notice the water gushing through the fissures that gave him support; he did not feel the scratch of rock on his cheek; and it was much later that he realized that the thin bleating he heard had come from his own mouth. All he was aware of was the weight of his stomach, the clanging in his head, and his unwieldy body that appeared to have been filleted of its bone and muscle and reduced to a limp bag. Until the hands that supported him were removed and he heard, "There you are. Made it," and he found himself standing on pebbles over which the water flowed shallowly and he saw the cliff curving around, its base near his feet. He wanted to thank Brocket, but he was choked with relief and the sudden invasion of air.

"When you're ready . . ." Brocket pulled at his socks. "These things are worse than sieves for holes."

At last Hilary managed, "Where next?"

For a time they walked beside the stream; the gorge was behind them, the cliffs growing lower. Then they reached a lane and as they turned east, Hilary said, "I'm not so bad climbing *up*."

Brocket laughed. "We're lucky, then. There's plenty of that ahead."

"It's just that, sometimes . . ." He wanted to explain.

"You got down. It's only a matter of practice."

"I hope you're right. It's worse when my imagination begins to work."

"I'll say."

"Does yours when you're climbing?"

"No. When I remember things I've been told. Stories. But I can't get away from them. Not like you. So it puzzles me why you tramp over these hills when you're taken like that."

"I have to finish what my father started." Hilary paused; his face twitched. "Dad was collecting material for a book on this part of the world."

And as they covered the next miles, panting over knolls, slithering down the banks of watercourses, striding along abandoned farm trails, Hilary told Brocket of his father's travels. He described his study of the great convulsions that had heaved the rocks into mountains and shot out the scalding lava; he explained the sliding and crashing of continents, the suck and flood of oceans and the shift of ice and desert as our planet rocked under the cascading sparks of the stars.

"Your dad must have been a real brainbox," Brocket commented. "Imagine passing all that on!" He was envious of Hilary's knowledge.

"Yes. But I didn't inherit his head for heights."

Hilary said no more, and glancing at his tense face, Brocket thought, Does he have to prove that he can do it, so as not to disappoint his father who is dead? I wonder what my dad, if I've got one, would think about me.

"Do you believe in ghosts?" he asked, but Hilary looked incredulous and shook his head.

They had reached another river, well east of the gorge. "Where exactly's your place, then?" Brocket asked.

"The other side of this river. Dad liked old lead mines and he made this one his base when he was researching in this area. He used it to store equipment and food, and he camped in it. But the school, where the books are, comes before that. It's in a village beyond this church in a field." He consulted the map. "Do you know it?"

"I know where the old school is."

"Good. Would you say the village is another three miles?"

"Thereabouts. But I need a snack."

"I need more than that." Hilary shared out chocolate and the thick, solid biscuit. Neither remarked that there was no food left. "I don't think we'll reach the mine this evening."

"We can try." But Brocket thought, Three miles to the library, then a further trek. Hilary's right; we'll be hard pressed to reach his store of supplies today; and if we don't, we shan't only be looking for medicines for Found, but for me. Food.

Then they set off again, able to walk faster than before because the path was by the side of the river and along easy, level ground. Now they were concentrating on their immediate goal.

"That old school's been locked up for years," Brocket remarked.

"Yes, but Dad told me about the books. I don't suppose it was worth anyone's trouble to clear them out."

They crossed over a suspension bridge, their feet resounding on the frozen planks, and came to a bend in the river.

"Look at that!"

"Where?"

Brocket pointed.

"You mean that green stuff?" Wedged into the riverbank, a fallen branch of alder had netted something in its twigs. Hilary peered. "I'm not wearing my glasses."

"It's a scarf."

"Yes?"

"It's new."

"It doesn't look very new to me."

"I mean new in the water."

"What makes you say that?"

"It isn't bashed around enough, is it? Bedraggled. If it'd been there awhile it'd have bits of weeds and leaves caught on it. It'd be thicker, be its own little weir, with the water swirling round it."

Hilary was impressed with the other's gift of observation. "I see."

"I'll tell you another reason I know that scarf's fresh there. Would you like to know it?"

"Go on."

"The reason is . . ." Brocket grinned. "It wasn't there last time I was passing."

Hilary laughed. "I asked for that!"

Brocket did not move on. "It's only recently dropped in and been stopped by that branch. Before it could be carried to the next bridge." He nodded downstream, the direction they were walking.

"What's the matter, Brocket?" Hilary asked, for the other's amusement had vanished; his face was somber. "Somebody has lost a scarf, that's all."

"Who, I wonder. Absconders and such don't use this path. They keep mainly to roads." He paused. "I wish it hadn't been this particular spot. Do you know what happened here?" Opposite them the bank of the river rose into a sharp cliff; a few shrubs and ferns striped the ledges, and along the crest were hawthorns and a solitary birch. "Years ago. After a long, long quarrel between two men. One was the doctor who attended folk in this valley. The other was a blacksmith and a drunk. He lived in the last village we went by and he was a sort of highwayman, a robber, besides being a blacksmith. The doctor didn't hide his opinion of him; he told the blacksmith that one day he would hang; and the blacksmith got mad and vowed he would stop the doctor's mouth. So he lay in wait and murdered him one night as he was riding through High Wood, then buried him. But he got scared that someone would find the grave, so he dug him up and carried him to this cliff and threw him into the river. It was the dead of night, but two people walking along this path heard the slap of the corpse in the water and followed it downriver till they could hook it out."

"What happened to the blacksmith?"

"He was hanged from the gibbet. But this was where he slung the body into the river. One black winter's night."

In the lee of the cliff the dusk was gathering, unchallenged by the low, pallid sun.

"It's only a scarf floating on the river," Hilary protested. "There's nothing else. Nobody has been pushed in."

Brocket was silent.

"It must have blown off."

Brocket gestured toward the cliff top. The graceful branches of the silver birch hung quiet and its delicate wisps of twigs were not stirred by the slightest breeze.

EIGHTEEN

For the next half mile they did not speak. Hilary wanted to argue. He wanted to say, It's ridiculous to suggest that two people could be thrown off the same cliff; the statistical probability must be one in millions. However, obeying Brocket's cautions, he kept quiet.

Then Brocket stopped. He asked, his voice low, "Did you see that? Going across the bridge."

Hilary peered over the other's shoulder and ahead of them to where the stone arches spanned the river. "What was it?"

"A combat vehicle."

"Really?"

"Look, there's another!" Brocket exclaimed. "Or is it?"

"No. Those are the communications boys. That truck's full of screens. The shield things on the roof are aerials."

"Here's something else. *This* looks nasty." The vehicle was a steel cube with no markings or external features, without windows or anything that resembled doors. Sliding noiselessly across the bridge, it was sleek and sinister in the dying light.

"The void patrol," Hilary murmured. "After street people on the run wanted for questioning."

"Or absconders."

They squatted under bushes and leaves of wild rhubarb.

"You've seen these operations before?" Hilary asked.

Brocket nodded. "A few. But not generally as late in the year. There aren't so many people getting out, trying their luck."

"I wonder how long they'll stay. We can't break into the school until they're gone."

"We don't have time to wait. There's not much light left and we need it." Brocket's words were almost inaudible as sirens blared near the bridge.

"I don't see how we can force a way in when all this is going on."

"We'll have to keep to the back."

There was a revving of engines, a rush of thudding boots, a rattle of shots, and a scatter of distant cries.

"Brocket, it's too dangerous to tackle this burglary now. Perhaps the void patrol will have gone by morning. If we tried at first light tomorrow, we could be on the road again nearly as soon as if we broke into the school now."

Brocket remembered the appearance of the baby. "It strikes me that we can't afford to lose an hour. How long do you think she's got?"

For a time there was no answer. At last Hilary said, "There's one advantage about that siren: it'll mask the sound of us bashing down doors."

They forced a way through the bushes, climbed a wall and up a small paddock. "We've come out just behind it," Brocket said. "There it is."

"It's exactly like Dad's description. And still standing."

"Not for many more years. See how the tiles are slipping? Soon as that starts, it's a goner. We'll try the windows first."

Cautiously, they thrust through nettles and overgrown plants, their boots crushing a few wrinkled currants the birds had left. At the end of the building was a door; it was made of oak and studded with iron nails.

"We could've done without the chains and padlocks," Brocket grumbled. "Those boards over the windows'll have to be ripped off."

"They don't go right to the top. Hang on." Gripping the edge of a board, kicking shallow dents for his toes into the warped surface, Hilary pulled himself up. His head bobbed; then he slithered down. "The panes are leaded; they could be pried out, but you need both hands."

"You heave me. I'm lighter than you."

Brocket took Hilary's jackknife, climbed up his back and onto his shoulders. He managed to open the lead, lift out the tiny panes, and pass them down. "Don't want to be heard dropping this glass," he murmured. Back on the ground, he asked, "Want to go first?"

"What about you?"

"Tie one of your ropes to the frame and I'll shinny up."

Suddenly, there was the pulse of the siren again, and engines erupted. They seemed to bear down on them, coming straight for the school yard.

"The road's close by, on the other side of the school," Brocket explained.

There was a shriek of brakes, the thud of a door, men's voices.

"Get up!" He was crouched, ready for Hilary's feet on his back.

Swaying on Brocket's shoulders, Hilary found that the light was too poor for him to tie the rope quickly, but after a struggle he managed to knot it around the frame. Meanwhile, from the front of the school came the sound of barking and the heavy pad of running dogs.

"Up!" He heard Brocket hiss and felt his feet being pushed. For a second he was raised higher. He grabbed at the stone wall, scrambled a knee onto a ledge, scraped it over and, straddling the windowsill, he looked down on Brocket. He was standing totally motionless, stretched against the wall.

Then at the corner of the building something moved into the low evening light, paws scuffed the ground, a powerful nose sniffed, found a fresh scent. Following it, a shape advanced. Groomed by the remnant of light, the hair shone glossy, the ears were pricked, the snout twitched, and eyes examined Brocket. But the dog appeared puzzled by the boy's stillness. It was accustomed to the panic of flight, to screams and commotion; it could see no racing legs around which to clamp locking jaws. The dog stepped closer and gave a short, testing growl.

Watching, Hilary thought, Should I slide back and help Brocket? But if I do, the men might get us both; one of us has to escape them; otherwise the baby will die.

Despite this sensible reasoning, Hilary was ashamed. Peering down from his safe position, he felt he was a coward.

He heard Brocket say, "There's a good boy," and, incredibly, to his ears came a short chuckle. The dog did not remove his eyes from Brocket, but his spine dipped slightly and his tail flicked.

"Good boy," Brocket repeated. "Home now. Home. Find."

The dog stood undecided. Barking was heard from the road. Reminded of duty, it tensed to jump. But there was a whistle. The poised head swayed, stretched forward; and the dog gave a hoarse bark into Brocket's face, then loped away.

Brocket did not move until the dog was around the corner of the building. "Now!" he hissed.

Hilary threw down the rope, saw the other grab it and begin to walk the wall, but before he reached the window, Hilary had squeezed back and was over the sill. Hanging from it, his legs dangling, he felt nothing but emptiness. Then the floor smacked his boots, throwing him into invisible objects; they slid and crashed, echoing, wood against wood. Immediately, the shouting outside halted, then began again, sharpened by purpose. Boots pounded, dogs yapped. Rope flopped at Hilary's feet and Brocket was whispering. "They'll search round the back and see the gap in the panes."

But the siren shrilled again from the bridge, and the boots and the clinks of metal and the raucous barking returned to the road. Not until the vehicle had started up, had roared after easier prey, did Hilary release his clutch on Brocket's arm and Brocket let the breath wheeze from his throat.

Disentangling themselves, they remained for a while crouched on the floor. At last Brocket said, "That was a close one."

"Not as close as that dog. It would have finished me off."

"It reckoned there was no use in starting on me. Not enough meat."

Then they were laughing, taking in great gulps of breath,

choking, rolling about on the floor and bumping into obstacles.

"These crates are bruisers," Brocket gasped.

"They're desks."

"Are they, now? Imagine sitting at them!"

It was almost dark, but they could make out enough to see that the room held only school furniture. Blundering through it, they found a door and beyond that, stairs. Above these was a room with unshuttered windows letting in the last light and the promise of stars. Here their feet slithered. They had found another obstruction. Paper. It covered the floor; it rose in gusts of white leaves as they stumbled through it, then it flapped down again, leaving the smell of mold in their nostrils and the taste of mice in their mouths.

"I suppose I shouldn't have expected anything else," Hilary said. "When you've got electronic data access, what's a book worth?"

"Are these them?"

"They were once. Before the vandals—patrolmen, I suppose—got to them. They tried burning them, too, only that's not such an easy task."

He nodded toward the hearth. In it, soft and feathery, was a heap of ashes. The remains of paper, fringed with scorch where the flames had bitten, clung to the soot lining the chimney; other sheets striped with yellow had drifted among the fire irons, poker, and tongs.

Scattered around the fireplace and occasionally forming rough piles were other objects that Brocket could not identify. He poked one gingerly, and his finger recoiled as the rotting thing gave way under his touch.

"Those are the covers and spines, after they tore out the pages. Do you know, Brocket, sometimes I think my dad is better off being out of it. He would have despaired if he'd seen this."

"There's a lot of damage," Brocket tried to sympathize. He knew that Hilary was expressing not only his father's feelings but his own. "I'll look, see if there's any left like they should be."

By then it was night. Darkness covered the room, but Brocket was used to it. Hands, fingertips, toes, and ears simply took over from eyes. He felt along the walls, found shelves and cabinets, heard their hollow answer to his questioning tap, continued until he reached a dais, climbed upon it, and discovered niches where his hands stroked surfaces that were polished and hard.

"I think I've turned some up," he shouted, and was rewarded by Hilary's relief.

However, Hilary could not examine the books then. He could not use his flashlight. Nor could they light a fire. The noise at the bridge still threatened.

The next morning, Brocket's first words were, "They've gone. Sometime in the dark. Did you hear?" Turning over, he saw that Hilary's sleeping bag was empty.

"We've been lucky," Hilary called from the dais. "Over here, there are lots of medical books. Only, the print is too small to read in this light."

"The sky's brightening. Listen to the birds."

"I hadn't noticed."

Brocket wondered how that was possible. "They're warning us to be off." The sooner we go, the sooner we get to Hilary's food, he said to himself, kneading his empty stomach. "It's a nice hearth. We could light a fire and warm up a meal if we had one."

Hilary shrugged away the fantasy and went on riffling through books.

Brocket dragged himself out of his bag. Where it had lain on the litter was a patchwork of torn pages.

"Did the school children read all these?" He could not imagine it.

"These aren't the sort of books they had in schools."

"But this was always a school, built centuries ago. A man left the village, made his fortune in the city, and came back and built the bridge, Mrs. Gimmer says. And this school for the children."

"I didn't know that." For a moment, his attention drawn from his research, Hilary looked up, examined the paneled walls, the huge hearth. "It's handsome. Plenty of space."

"I reckon I'd rather be outside."

Hilary allowed his eyes to travel over the floor. The devastation was clearer and looked more shocking in the growing light. "These books belonged to a man who made this part into his library after the school was closed."

"Did he read them all?"

"Perhaps. How should I know?" Hilary was impatient with this unanswerable question. "Look, I've just turned up a medical dictionary and identified Found's symptoms. I want to jot down the treatment." He took out his notebook. "Won't be long."

Brocket walked along the shelves of elegant volumes. He wanted to examine them but felt timid. Books were foreign things and daunting, full of hard words. But at last he took one down. Gently he smoothed his fingers down the gilt edges and the leather spine, where the titles were worked in gold. Opening it, he admired the marbled endpapers, turned the pages and found pictures painted in delicate pastels. They were protected by tissue paper, transparent and frail. Opposite them was a mass of indecipherable print, but one of the pictures was of two children walking through a forest. They looked lost but seemed to be following a trail of pebbles, which shone under the moon. The girl reminded him of Ren. She would like this, he said to himself and, disregarding its weight, he managed to wedge the book inside the lining of his parka and pulled the belt tight.

"Ready?" Hilary shouted.

Dawn had now slid down the hills and established itself in the village. They descended from the library, used desks to climb up to the hole they had made in the window, returned to the river path, and having made sure that the road was empty of patrolmen, they crossed over William Craven's bridge.

NINETEEN

Brocket said, "Now, which of the old lead mines is your base in?" His arm made a great swooping arc. "You've plenty to pick from."

"I haven't approached it from this direction before." Hilary consulted his map. "About four miles by road, but there may be a shortcut. Here's the place." He put a finger on the spot.

"I don't have much to do with maps." By which he meant: nothing. However, under Hilary's guidance, he soon learned. "Right. We'll cut straight across. It's steep, but not difficult. This is a stream, isn't it? This blue line? And we're aiming beyond it, to here? *Here?*"

"Yes."

Carefully, feeling his chest tighten, Brocket scrutinized the map, related the position to the one on the ground. Why, of all places that Hilary's father could have chosen, had he hit upon *this?* "It's a bit off the way I generally go." He hoped that his voice did not betray him. "I'm not sure of the paths."

Hilary lined up north on the map with the compass needle, found their position, placed the compass on it, and read the direction to his cache. "It's east-northeast."

Brocket looked at the little instrument, trying to distract himself. "That's clever."

"It's only magnets." He did not seem to remember that he had given Brocket a compass he could not set.

"This one has a little light in it. See, it works from the heat of your hand. It'll be useful if we need it on the way back."

"Not if it's my hands round it." Already they had turned into icicles. He tucked them into his pockets. "But we won't have to move in the dark. If we step on it, we'll be there within an hour and a half. So we can be away long before dusk."

"Heavens! I certainly hope so."

"These parts can be nasty, at night."

"Nasty? You mean, dangerous?" Hilary was thinking about cliffs, holes, bogs, and sudden chasms; he had not heard Brocket's special apprehension. "We'll have to carry on, whether it's dark or light."

"Is the baby as bad as that?"

"She needs antibiotics. The most she's got is another day."

After that answer, the tightness in Brocket's chest twisted further, becoming a dense knot.

Following the route they had chosen, and guided by the compass, they came near their goal in the estimated time.

"It's close; on our right," Hilary directed as they strode along a sunken road. It was rutted by carts that had once carried away the lead. "I suppose, when they were working this seam there would be dozens of men milling about, and horses and the sound of pumps and all that. It doesn't seem right, does it, without people and noise?"

Brocket agreed. Here men had taken over the hillsides, had dug and tunneled, had brought up stone, ground it, and sieved out the lead; and the heaps of dross, which were now grassy humps, and the drifts of grit and the rusted wheels were all that was left. It was a dreary, abandoned place. With its memories, it was more lonely than the vast undisturbed spaces of the echoing hills.

"There it is." Hilary pointed to an opening roofed by an arch of hewn rock and filled by a rough barrier of stones. This was the entrance to a worked seam.

"It's a pity your dad couldn't find somewhere else. There're enough empty farms around."

"I told you. He liked the old lead mines."

I bet he didn't know about It, Brocket said to himself, looking along the track. At the bottom, hidden from view by a spur of cliff, ran a stream; where It stalked.

They climbed to the entrance of the mine. In front of it the soil was moist and newly turned. Brocket groaned. It's like a heap left by Something digging, digging out what It has buried, he told himself.

"This is odd," Hilary said. "I didn't leave the ground like this. Someone's been here. It can't be the fellow who brings batteries and things. He leaves everything as he found it."

Brocket wanted to tell him: We're very close. Hundreds of people have seen It. Mrs. Gimmer says the miners never walked home alone.

"I wouldn't object to anyone using the place to shelter in, but I don't want the equipment tampered with."

Still talking, not seeing the hand that Brocket shot out to prevent him, Hilary squeezed through a small gap between stones and into the mine. Brocket waited for the screams and the crunching of monstrous jaws, but all he heard was a startled murmur.

"It's Raymond," Hilary shouted. "The man I've just mentioned."

So, for the moment relieved, Brocket joined him. Little light penetrated the slim gap, but he could make out Hilary and, finally, bunched at his feet, a heap of sodden clothes.

"I can't get a word of sense out of him," Hilary said.

There was a weak jerk as his hand touched the man's jacket, an intake of breath and a moan. The head turned and a face looked up. "Don't!"

They peered at the drawn mouth and the blanched skin. "Ray, what the hell has happened?"

The lips tried to smile, abandoned the effort, and whispered, "You sound like your dad."

"We've got to get him out of those clothes," Brocket said.

He heard a click, and above him an electric lamp bobbed. He was standing in a wide passage. Its sides, cut by picks, were vertical; its ceiling was jagged, supported by pillars and beams; its floor was uneven, a bed for chips of shale and the rust-colored stone. These were washed shallowly by drips of water, which fell rhythmic and sharp. That was how, over a century before, it had been left by the miners. Now it held plastic chests, cans of food, drums of water, a ladder, tools, and ropes. To Brocket's amazed eyes, its treasures were infinite: a washbowl fixed to a tripod, a metal plate on which stood pans, a hammock slung from a beam, a web of cables from which radiated wires to boxes that hummed.

He remarked, "Your father meant business."

"He was thorough." Hilary pulled blankets out of a steel trunk.

Promising himself an exhaustive inspection later, Brocket knelt by Raymond. "He needs heat."

"I've got a heater, but I'd rather not switch it on if we can avoid it; it uses so much juice."

The man muttered, "Don't you bother. The blankets will suffice. You just lay them on." He seemed not to have understood their intention to remove his wet clothing, and when Hilary tried to peel off his jacket he recoiled. "Leave it!"

"You'll grow worse lying in it."

"It's the handling. I wouldn't be surprised if that shoulder was gone."

"We'll be careful."

"I'm telling you to leave off!" But this attempt at authority was fruitless, and he was left grumbling, "It's two against one."

"That's right."

It took them some time to undress him. His body was unwieldy, a clumsy dead weight, and one arm swung and poked at an abnormal angle. As they took off the jacket, body warmer, and jersey, he cried out. But once that was over, he became easier.

Hilary asked, "Can you manage something to eat, Ray?"

"I'd give it a try."

So Hilary switched on the electric hotplate, selected packets, and mixed the contents into a thick soup. Meanwhile Brocket, bewildered by choice, dithered over the cans. "Yan, tyan, tethera, methera, pimp, sethera, lethera, othera, dothera, deek, yandeek, tyandeek, tetheradeek, metheradeek, bumfit," he chanted.

"Whatever's that?" Hilary demanded. "Sounds like a spell."

"Mrs. Gimmer taught me. It's the way shepherds used to count sheep."

"I'd be grateful if you would teach me."

"Not before I've had a taste of that soup, I hope," said Raymond. Its smell was enough to begin his recovery. "I'm ready for it."

"We've been ready for days."

Even so, they forced themselves not to eat until they had fed Raymond. With the right arm useless and the other weak and quivering, he could not get the food into his mouth without spilling. Hilary supported him while Brocket spooned it up, feeling shy at performing such a service for a grown man. As his mouth opened, his tongue licked, and his throat swallowed, he reminded Brocket of Found. Surely babies don't die; die, just like that? he said to himself. Surely she'll hold out till night or early morning tomorrow?

But, at last permitted to eat, he began to feel more optimistic. The food slid down his gullet, spread warmth and energy inside his chest, and he assured himself, She'll be fine; and Lil and Ren'll have as good a feast as this.

"After that, I reckon I'll get through the night," Raymond announced, though his smile became a grimace at another stab of pain.

"The problem is, Ray, we can't stay with you."

"I don't expect it."

"We're pressed for time. I'll leave you water and some soup in this thermos flask." Hilary was brisk, moving on to the next job.

Brocket objected. "We can't leave him here like this!"

"Can you suggest an alternative?"

Lying between them, the man muttered, "I'll manage. I won't start to worry till I hear myself raving."

"He's in agony with that arm and he's running a temperature. Just think what it's like to be left alone in that state."

Angry, Hilary blushed. "I believe I can imagine it. I don't need to be prompted. So what do we do? Go on, you tell me. It's him or Found."

"It doesn't need two of us to take the medicine." Disappointed, Brocket thought, We set out together; we've shared every minute so far. I wanted us to finish it the same way. And then I'd be able to say: Once I knew a young fellow, older than me and with schooling, and him and me together we did something important. We fetched medicines for a baby.

Hilary was staring at him. "Very well." His voice was tight. "You stay with Raymond." He thought, If I come to another ravine I won't have him to help me, but at least I'll know that once I conquered one.

"No. I'll take the stuff. I'll be there sooner." Perhaps, Brocket encouraged himself silently, It won't be lurking; there isn't a full moon.

"You don't know how to give an injection."

"Do you?"

"I've watched."

"Don't trouble yourselves over me," Raymond interrupted. "Soon as I've had a few hours of decent sleep, I'll be able to go."

"To go!" Brocket exclaimed. "You're too weak to *crawl.*"

"You shouldn't talk like that. I got here, didn't I?" Holding in the groans, the man raised himself on his uninjured arm. "You try covering the miles soaked through and with a crippled shoulder after you've been forced off a cliff by dogs and left for dead in the river. How many would have managed that? You name them."

"You were forced off the cliff?" Brocket echoed. "Where the blacksmith threw down the doctor?"

"Yes. The dogs had me in a circle. I hadn't a chance."

"They found Brocket later."

He corrected: "Only the one."

"Well, this was the whole pack," Raymond said. "I thought I was done for when they closed in. They were surprised when I jumped." Briefly invigorated by the memory, he chuckled. "I remember the look on the face of one as I went over—disappointed. They set up a howling and ran about, peering over the edge, but not a one of them tried to leap down. Been bred ferocious, but they haven't lost their natural sense."

"But the water's low, and there the riverbed is nothing but plates and rock."

"There was a branch of alder handy for landing on. When the patrol caught up, they decided the only thing left with any life in it was my scarf."

"We saw it yesterday evening."

"It's been there a day or two. Like I was, till the chance came to move. I didn't want it known I was hereabouts. It's not in my interests at the moment to be answering questions."

Hilary raised an eyebrow but did not ask him to explain. Instead: "It's a wonder you haven't caught pneumonia. I'll stay with you. You wouldn't be in this state if you hadn't been bringing me supplies."

"I hadn't any on me. That's not why I'm here. There's nothing you can do, except try strapping me up. Then when I've got rid of the shakes, I can move on and finish what I came for. You see . . ." he paused for a moment. "You see, I had a message to find an absconder."

"What?"

"Despite Security being on a mopping-up job, I had to get past. I was in haste. Winter's coming early, and it can finish refugees off more quickly than patrolmen can."

"I didn't know you helped absconders," Hilary said.

"Now and again. Your father was in on it, naturally."

"He didn't tell me."

"He would've when he saw fit. Me delivering stuff here acts as a handy cover when I'm sent on a search."

Hilary was trying to absorb this new image of his father. To him, he had been a geologist, a scholar, an organizer, a man physically fearless, aware of little other than his work. "So Dad helped absconders?"

"Street people as well. Your father was independent in more ways than one." Hilary caught Brocket's eye. They were thinking of Lil. "Anyway, he reckoned most folks are better off in the provinces farther north, not so many rules and regulations. And there's a home waiting for this one."

Brocket asked, "What's this absconder's name?"

"I've forgotten it for the moment. Something to do with trees."

"Look, Brocket," Hilary interrupted, "would you choose some packets and cans? The girls will be starving. And there's soup—I made plenty—which is for them as well. It'll stay warm in that thermos. I'll look for the antibiotics. They should be in the fridge. I'd be surprised if Dad hadn't stocked any."

As, busy and efficient, Hilary turned away, Raymond grumbled, "This chill's frozen my memory, but when I was told the name of the absconder I had to find, I remember thinking, And I've got to look for her! Shy, keeping out of sight!"

"That doesn't sound like a tree. Could the name be Ren?" Brocket held his breath.

"You've got it! Wren. Knew it had to do with trees. Well, bushes; but, still, I was close. You'd expect to remember such a name without any trouble and I had in my mind a *bird,* but it made me think of . . ."

He would have continued to ramble on, but Brocket was calling, "Hilary, he's looking for Ren."

His words were loud and excited, but the hewn walls sent back an echo that was cracked and dissonant, and Brocket thought, Shouldn't I be glad?

TWENTY

They got through their exclamations; they listened to Raymond's account of the people who helped absconders, any homeless on the run; they told him their story. They arranged when he should go get Ren and he promised to find someone to foster Found. "I reckon Greta will take her, along with the young girl," he said. "Sounds like that baby's in a bad way. You get those antibiotics to her quick. You can leave off tending to me."

They did not need to be urged. They were already packed. Silently they had agreed to remain together for the return.

Raymond's good-bye was: "You're in for a long hike, but if your legs don't give up you might reach those girls by morning."

"We'll try."

But when they stepped out of the mine, they saw that

there was little daylight left. "The going's a little bit rough for a mile or two; then we reach a road," Brocket said. Before then, they would have to walk through Its favorite haunt. The slopes were in shadow. The entrances to the mine shafts were black caverns. Stones creaked under his boots like discarded bones. "I don't like this place," he told Hilary.

"I think it's interesting. There's a wonderful view from here. Look. Behind you."

Brocket had no intention of looking behind.

Because It always followed. It never appeared from the side. It always stalked in Its quarry's own shadow, close, out of sight.

And the dread of that did not lessen when they reached the road. However much Brocket hurried, he could not shake it off; the creature continued to pace itself to his steps.

"Would you mind slowing down a bit?" Hilary puffed. "You must have bellows for lungs."

"We can't afford to dawdle."

"There isn't any danger of that. More likely we'll take off. Two deafening explosions and we'll be streaking away, a couple of trails of exhaust and two scorched knapsacks orbiting the earth."

"Don't waste breath. We have to get as far as we can before dark."

The night was approaching fast now; the remnant of daylight was hooded by clouds. Below them the road was a passage where little light poked through the raftering branches.

Hilary remarked, "At this pace, we'll be on the Monks' Way in a couple of hours."

It won't hound me along that road, Brocket assured himself. It dare not trespass there. Its evil shrinks before the power of those righteous ghosts. Once I have reached the Monks' Way, I am safe. Despite his protesting muscles, he quickened his pace.

Hilary stated, "I have to rest soon."

"Not yet."

We must keep on, he urged himself silently. We can't stop. We must stay ahead of It. We must gain that road's sanctuary. If It guesses our goal, It will close in. And as he permitted that thought, Brocket sensed it was answered. Behind him there was a sound, a low, warning bay. "Can't you walk faster?" he demanded.

"No. This is stupid. We have miles yet."

"Didn't you hear something?"

"What?"

"Listen. A bark."

"My ears are bursting with this rush. Could it be patrol dogs? Have they come back?"

"It's not them."

"How can you be sure?"

"Not that kind of noise."

"What, then, a fox?"

"It's getting nearer."

"You hear better than I do."

Brocket pretended to glance over his shoulder. "You have a look."

"Can't see anything. Too dark."

It was never too dark for It to see you, caught in the hot beams of its eyes. They pierced into your back and spun you around while your legs were thrashed by the whipping chains. He could hear those now. They were slicing through the hedgerow and grinding over the pebbles of the road.

"You wouldn't see a fox, anyway," Hilary told him.

The chains swung in great swaths but did not hinder the speed of the creature's pursuit.

"A fox doesn't follow humans. There's no danger of attack," Hilary objected as Brocket began to run.

"We must reach the Monks' Way." It was drawing closer. Panting. Not because It was tired and weakening. Because It was impatient. Eager for the kill. "Can't you hear It?"

"No."

"You're making too much noise."

"Brocket, stop! What are you frightened of?"

"This is where It comes."

"It?"

"Barguest." He had named it. That was a mistake. It would think It was being called.

"What's that?"

"A dog."

"A *dog?*"

"Yes."

"Brocket, you're not running away from a *dog?*"

"I have to."

"But . . . yesterday . . . you faced the one on patrol."

"This is different."

"It couldn't be more fierce."

"It's a killer."

"We can deal with it. There are two of us."

"No matter. It would get me. It's on my scent."

"So was the other. You weren't afraid of him."

"This attacks from behind."

"There's nothing behind us. Brocket, are you running away from a *ghost?*"

"Worse."

"Tell me."

"Save breath."

"Stop, Brocket! Look! You'll see there is nothing."

The shafts of the eyes drill into your head; they blind you to all but the gleaming points of the teeth, the saliva frothing over the gums, the steaming lash of the tongue. Then the forelegs leap and your chest is impaled on the daggers of claws. "If you look, you're done for."

"You've *got* to look. You have to see there is nothing following us. Otherwise, you are truly done for."

The words came in great, sucking pants and were overtaken by others loud in his ears. A paw gripped his arm. Claws scored, ripped the flesh, hooked out muscles and bone while his skull was tossed, pounded and cracked on stone like a snail by a thrush. Then the mouth burrowed, obscenely nuzzling. His brain split and was scattered by gnashing jaws.

"Brocket." Hilary's voice was anxious; his hand was searching Brocket's face, feeling over his head. Above, through the layers of branches, there was a slim stripe of sky. "Can you sit up?"

Grit pressed through the fabric of his parka, hurting his elbows. As he raised his shoulders, he was deafened by the drumming in his head.

"I didn't mean to knock you down," Hilary apologized. "Is anything broken?"

"I don't think so." Along the surface of the road, the wind skimmed icily, but his clothes were damp with sweat. Attempting to rise, he discovered that his legs trembled.

"You'll be fine in a moment. Panic's over." And Hilary added carefully, "I don't particularly enjoy traveling in the dark, either. It makes stretches like this so enclosed."

"It's only in this part that I'm bothered."

"I see."

Brocket thought, I shouldn't be lying here talking. It could pounce any minute. But with Hilary kneeling over him, that did not seem so likely. In any case, he argued, Barguest would have to champ his way through Hilary first. Almost amused, he added: It would find him tough.

Hilary asked,"Are there many of these animals around?"

"Just the one."

"What's the incidence of its appearance?"

"It's enormous, and black and Its eyes . . ."

"I meant, how often is it spotted?"

"It's been stalking people for years. The miners saw It. They say It was the only thing that could scare that blacksmith."

"Didn't you say he was a drunkard? That's hardly our problem. Also, if this Barguest has been around so long, he's a great age—centuries old—and too decrepit to do much harm. He would be no match for us, especially when we stared him straight in the face." He twisted Brocket around. The road was empty.

"All the same," Hilary added, "I might feel uneasy if I walked this road in the dark by myself. Come on." He bent down, groped, and found Brocket's hand. "What's this?" he asked, a finger searching his companion's palm.

"A scratch."

"It feels deeper than a scratch."

"The buckle on one of your boots did it."

"I haven't had them off." Then, "I see. It seems years since you were taking me down that gorge."

When Brocket was on his feet, Hilary joked, "Have to keep a check on your pulse." And not until they were out of the corridor of trees, had passed by dense woods, did Hilary loosen his hold on Brocket's wrist.

They stopped once. Though the Monks' Way was straight and open and permitted a reasonably fast pace, they had to rest.

"Guess how long we've been walking." Hilary looked at his watch.

"If you tell me, my legs'll think it's time to give up."

"Mine already do."

"They might strengthen after a cup of that soup."

When they had drunk some, Brocket said, "It's only another couple of hours away. Can we do it?"

"We'd get it to her by dawn. Those few hours might be crucial."

"That settles it, then."

Their legs ached; their feet were swollen lumps that at every step were ready to burst out of their boots. Their stomachs pitched and rolled; their minds sagged. Never before had either walked such a distance uninterrupted. Brocket reminded himself, It's no farther than Mrs. Gimmer could manage and, straightening, he gripped the straps of his pack.

Hilary said, "We're lucky my father stocked a good range of medicines."

"Let's hope they're in time."

It was that thought that obsessed them during the last miles. The rest was unimportant. Hilary's fear of heights became a transitory handicap; Barguest slunk away, a creature vanquished if challenged. In their dizzy and misting vision, all they saw was the white, unstirring face of Found.

At last they ran along the path that led up to the trailer. "We'll scare them stiff," Brocket panted, "arriving in the dark."

However, he was wrong. A voice reached them: "I thought I heard you."

"We've brought food, medicines."

"I think they're too late," Ren said.

TWENTY-ONE

When they climbed into the trailer, Brocket was struck by the smell. It was sour and musty, and after hours in the crisp night air, he thought he would choke. He felt that he was entering a place where no breeze or draft had penetrated; it was as if the trailer was a closed, windowless tomb.

"I think we should have a light," he heard Hilary say.

A flashlight clicked, and its beam arched over the damp hay, over the packs lolling among their scattered contents, over the carriage stained with used diapers and the last, empty cans. In a corner of this neglect was a sleeping bag. Lil lay in it, an arm raised against the light.

"Where is she?"

Lil felt for the zip of the bag, but her former deftness had vanished. Snagging and fumbling, her fingers were old and sick.

Brocket said to himself, Is she weak from starving, or is it something else? Aloud, he offered, "Let me," and Lil did not refuse him.

Inside the bag, stretched at Lil's side, was Found. The light drew nearer, found the woolen bonnet, edged down the clammy forehead, and touched the closed, sunken eyes. The lids did not flicker. Neither did the mouth open nor bubble out a protesting moan.

"She's been like this for . . . I can't remember." Ren spoke with difficulty.

"Is she drinking?"

"Not much . . . I don't know. Lil had some glue-something."

"Glucose?"

"Yes."

"That would help." Hilary began to search with his flashlight. "Where's that lantern you had?" The one that Annie Gimmer had sent to guide them through the railroad tunnel. Dully aware that she should assist, Ren groped among the mess of their baggage. Her movements were jerky and feeble.

Brocket knelt to help her. He wanted to explain: We've been walking all night; we're finished; nobody could've been any quicker. Instead, he said, "She could still live."

Turning to him, Ren shook her head, and watched a tear drip down his face. Her own was stiff and dry; her crying was done.

When they had lit the candle in the lantern, Hilary opened his knapsack and took out the medicines he had brought. "Antibiotic," he explained the slim packet. "It has to be injected."

Ren did not move. Lil placed a hand on Found's head. In the quiet glow of the lantern, her eyes were expressionless.

Hilary whispered to Brocket, "This gives me the creeps. What shall we do?"

"Is there any use now?"

"How can I know? We haven't been all that way, gone through"—for a moment he paused—"all that, to give up without trying. If we don't even try, we might as well have not bothered."

"But if she's dead . . . we can't . . . I mean, stick a needle . . . if she is . . ."

"Stop saying that!" Hilary's voice rose, querulous with desperation. "An injection can't do any harm. Whether or not. Anyway, we haven't looked." He bent down and lifted away Lil's hand. Poking among the child's clothing, he found a wrist. "I can't detect any pulse," he reported, "but my hands are so cold they've lost all feeling. Lil, won't you sit up? Unwrap her a bit so that I can listen at her chest."

Lil did not stir.

Brocket came forward, squatted by the side of Lil's sleeping bag, and lifted the child onto his lap. Her body was limp and sagged against him. "Ren!" he pleaded.

"I can't," she whispered.

Therefore, nervous and uncertain, Hilary and Brocket opened zippers and buttons, raised the shirt and vest. Underneath, the body was wasted, ridged by the hoops of ribs. Hilary put down his head. "I can't be sure. There may be a beat." Clumsily, he stuffed the undergarments into the leggings. "Can you take off that top thing, Brocket? We need to get at an arm."

By this time Brocket was past objections. Already, lifting Found, nursing her, he had schooled himself not to think of her as a corpse because otherwise he could not have done it. He said to himself, When you're dead you go stiff and she isn't stiff, just a bit floppy, like a bag without bones; she isn't *stiff*. In this way he had overcome his nausea, and his head did not spin when, following Hilary's request, he took hold of the sleeves of the coat and the woolen sweater and withdrew an arm.

"Hold it," Hilary ordered, and Brocket supported the stick of arm on his hand.

Hilary opened a packet, pulled out a wad of cotton, moistened it with liquid from a bottle, and dabbed it above the thin elbow. The vapor from the spirit rose, scraped their throats, and spreading inside the trailer, cleansed the fetid air.

"The needle is sterilized." He broke open another packet, removed a syringe, and thrust the point into a capsule. "It said this is the dose for her age," he murmured as he siphoned off half. The measure rose up the plastic cylinder.

"It's ready," Hilary announced, and looked toward Lil, but she did not move. He turned to Ren and saw her fists tight by her sides, her eyes pinched closed. "Lil?" he prompted again, but there was no answer.

Hilary knelt there, the syringe lying in his palm. Brocket, his eyes on it, waiting, saw it begin to quiver. "You do it," Hilary begged.

Brocket gasped. "I don't know how."

"I'll keep the place steady."

"I'm holding her. I don't have a free hand."

"You can give her to me."

Found seemed to be moving. "Is she waking up?" Brocket asked before he saw that it was his own hand that was causing the bared arm to shake. "I can't do it," he moaned.

"Take it. Please. I'll guide you."

"I'm exhausted. I can't see straight."

"The same goes for me."

Brocket thought, This is worse for him than when he was climbing down the gorge. "We'd better have a rest. After that, we'll manage."

"She can't wait."

Then Ren left her corner. She came like an animal crawling, her head bent. "Show me," she croaked, and picked up the syringe. "Put it there."

Hilary placed the point. "You push on the plunger when you've got the needle in," he told her.

The baby was propped against Brocket's chest; her arm was held, helpless in Hilary's grasp; the skin lay ready for the needle's prick.

Ren's face was ashen. The shadows thrown by the lantern renewed the bruises on her chin and pried out a nerve that ticked. This disappeared and her jaw tightened. For a second the fingers around the syringe conquered their quaking, jabbed, were halted by the sensation of the point entering, then a thumb pressed down. The child did not flinch.

"That's fine," Hilary breathed. "Keep your thumb there till it's all gone in."

"You tell." The words were almost inaudible. Ren was looking beyond Brocket's shoulder. She could not lower her eyes to glimpse what her fingers performed.

"It's finished," Hilary informed her when all the liquid had descended and vanished into the arm. He eased the syringe away.

The child remained motionless. She must be dead, Brocket decided, because he had told himself that if Found were still alive, she would immediately react. "That proves it," he said.

Hilary demanded, "Proves what?"

Ren's posture had not changed. She was crouched between

them, her hand stretched out but empty now. "It was no use," she echoed Brocket's deduction. Her body folded, her arms fluttered, and slithering down, she came to rest, insensible, beside Found's meager chest.

Brocket could not work out afterward how he and Hilary had managed, though from the evidence next morning he knew what they had done. When he woke, Ren was asleep in her bag and the baby's head lay beside Lil's. But he did no more than glance at Found; he did not listen for breathing. In the chill dawn he did not wish to risk learning that the antibiotic had not arrived in time. And his stomach was demanding food. "In my knapsack," he ordered his legs and levered himself up.

On his feet, he could not straighten and the tilt of the floor seemed steeper than the sides of the gorge. The two yards to the pack were longer than the miles they had walked the previous night. Along the route were scattered packets, a half-empty capsule, and a discarded syringe. His groping hands, unmanageable, knocked over a lantern in which a bristle of wick was preserved in a solid puddle of wax. And when at last he reached the knapsack, his eyes, still misty, did not scrutinize it, nor did his dizzy brain puzzle over what it held. The goat's milk with the skin from boiling slid like liquid satin down his throat, and the chunks of roasted rabbit rolled fragrant over his tongue. When he returned to his bag, his body was still heavy but stronger and he passed into tranquil sleep.

He would have continued all day had not Hilary roused him. "It's time for another injection. I suppose you'd better eat first."

"I already have."

"So have we." Although Hilary was pale, the food and rest had restored him and he was brisk, hopeful.

Encouraged, Brocket asked, "Is the antibiotic working?"

"She's definitely breathing, and there seems to be more life in her than there was in the night."

That was true also of Ren and Lil. They were sitting at the door of the trailer. Behind them were opened cans, scraped clean, and now they were finishing off the soup that had been brought in the thermos.

"There hasn't been a squeak from them for ages," Hilary said. "Open a can and they go mad."

Found lay curled in a nest of hay lined with a rag of blanket. It was difficult to determine exactly the change in her, but it was definitely there. Peering at her, Brocket decided that this had something to do with her skin. It looked less spongy.

He watched Hilary prepare the syringe and asked, "Who's doing it?"

"Ren says she will." Hilary lowered his voice. "Brocket, be warned. I think Lil's gone a little crazy."

"She looks the same to me."

"It's her manner. Anyway, Ren's taken this on. She seems quite eager, I suppose because the baby is not . . . There's a chance that Found will survive."

The injection went more smoothly this time, and although her eyes were blinking, Ren dared to look.

After that, Brocket made a fire and they boiled water Hilary fetched from the stream. "Dehydration is the real danger—being dried up," he told them. "So we have to get liquid into her."

"That's what Annie Gimmer said."

Brocket exclaimed, "Mrs. Gimmer's been *here?*"

"Yes."

"Why?"

Ren murmured, "She's been searching for Cob."

Brocket nodded. "I hope you told her Cob gave up the hunt. Mrs. Gimmer's been tramping around for days. When was it, Hilary, that you came across her?"

Hilary closed his eyes and tried to recall the occasion. "I know it was before we discovered Found was ill. Of course! I met her the same evening I found you in the shippon; I was going back for the cart. Perhaps it was a week ago?" He frowned, calculating. "Good heavens, no! It's less than four days."

"I'm stumped over why she came as far south as this." Momentarily, Brocket admired his knowledge of the compass. "She's old. Nowadays she doesn't journey farther down than the head of the river. What did she say?" he asked Ren.

"There was something she wanted to find out," Ren stammered, aware of Lil's agitation.

"What was that?"

But he was not answered. Lil moaned, pushed herself from their circle, and scrambled toward her sleeping bag. There she stretched out, her back turned to them and an arm over her face.

Brocket's eyes followed her, but his mind was on Annie Gimmer. He remembered his breakfast of goat's milk and meat. "Mrs. Gimmer gave you food. I ate it. Why didn't you? You were half-starving."

"Lil couldn't face it, and I couldn't, either. Every time we tried, we remembered what she'd said about Cob."

Brocket hardly heard her answer. He had recalled something else. "Mrs. Gimmer left her pack."

"She said she had no use for it anymore."

"I see." He got up. "I've got to go to her."

Hilary tried to restrain him. "You need more rest. You may have to hike miles."

"Not many. I know where she'll be. It's no more than an hour away, due south of here."

"I'll come with you."

"You can't, Hilary. There's Found."

"I'll come soon, then. Where to?"

Brocket was already out of the trailer and making for the path. "A cave at the foot of a long cliff." That was where she had said he must lay her.

"How do you know she'll be there?"

"Where else would she go when she'd given away her food and left her pack?" he shouted, and began to run.

Ren called after him, "Don't you want your knapsack?"

But Brocket ignored her. He was listening to Annie's instructions: "You bury me in that cave." And her grim joke: "That is, if I go first."

"You don't have to stay to help with the next injection," Ren told Hilary. "I can manage it. Will you leave me your watch?"

He fastened it round her wrist, where it slid about, as loose as a bangle. "Don't forget the water. Try to get some into her."

"Yes."

As Hilary fastened up his jacket and gathered up his equipment, he told her, "I must confess I'm totally at sea. What's the mystery? Why?" He nodded toward Lil.

Ren gestured a warning and led him out. "Annie Gimmer was certain that Cob is dead, and she seemed to think it was Lil's fault," she began.

Despite Ren's precautions, Lil heard her whispers. For a few minutes she lay on her sleeping bag, her mind clanging with Annie Gimmer's words. However much she concentrated her eyes on the roof or the patch of sky at the door, she could not see them. They were covered with pictures of a lantern's beam rushing down a rock-toothed passage, of a bundle placed between roots, of a black coat skimming the frost-pearled grass and a gaunt face turned to challenge. With a tearless sob, she rose, knelt by Found, drew a finger down a cheek, then slithered toward Brocket's pack.

Just as she had checked the contents of Ren's knapsack, so she went through this, arguing to herself, It must be here; I've looked everywhere else. Then she sighed, satisfied, as digging right to the bottom, her fingers found the knife. Pulling it out, she weighed it in her palm, tested her grip on the handle, and touched the needle-sharp point. Silently she rejoiced at possessing a thing so efficient and suited to her purpose. But it bore a blemish. Iridescent in the dim light, a stain ran down the length of the blade. Puzzling, Lil held it closer; then, with an exclamation of disgust, she spat on the hem of a skirt and cleaned away this last remnant of Cob's blood.

TWENTY-TWO

Outside, having set his course, Hilary told Ren, "I don't imagine it'll be long before we're back."

It was embarrassing, the way she wanted to smile when she should be thinking about their search for Annie Gimmer.

"Sure you'll be able to cope? You may have to deal with everything since Lil is so—how shall I put it?—unpredictable."

"I'll be fine." She wanted him to go. She could not restrain the laughing much longer. "If you hurry, you might catch up to Brocket." She wished she could give him a push.

"Not much hope of that. He doesn't have legs. He has pistons."

And when at last Hilary did leave her, she waited until he had disappeared over a knoll before she let the gladness flow. Listening to what he had told her, she had held her hands tightly behind her to prevent her arms rotating like propellers. But now she could release them and she could let her feet dance and her legs kick and her throat spill out the laughter. Although Found's illness was not over and Lil was strange and Brocket was imagining the worst for Annie Gimmer, her fortunes were improving. Her own fortunes, hers, Ren's. Someone was coming for her. The moment that Hilary had said, "Oh, Ren, there's something I've forgotten to tell you," she had known what it was going to be. He had apologized: "We were so tired, and busy with Found as soon as we got back, and you passed out and then this morning I didn't remember because, well, there was so much to do." But at last he had given her the news.

After it, everything was different. The sky was not so lofty; it did not dwarf her. The clouds frothed but did not shut away the sun. The wind did not scrape but tapped on her cheeks. Around her, the land was no longer hostile. White rocks in the distance glittered and winked. Nearer, leaves fell from a tree like fluttering moths. The last berries swung on a bush, resembling glowing scarlet beads.

Invigorated, flushed, Ren entered the trailer. "Lil, guess who Hilary and Brocket have met," she called.

But Lil's answer was, "Go away!"

"Lil," she shouted again as she saw the slim blade of metal poised over a wrist; and she was leaping forward, was down on a struggling body, was fighting for the hand, was sinking her teeth in the knotted fingers and prying away the knife. Immediately, the flesh of a palm opened, red spurted, and Lil was screaming, "Give it back!" Fists beat at her chest; feet kicked her legs. Then she was standing under the sky, where blood, strangely warm, spotted her face as she raised her arm, turned it around and around like a wheel, and sent the dripping knife from her hand to curve up, before dropping into bracken, to be buried at the roots.

"Curse you," Lil yelled behind her. She jumped down from the trailer, her eyes on the path the knife had taken.

"Leave it," Ren ordered, and made a grab.

Lil flung Ren's hand away, saw the blood fly and its print on her sleeve. "You're cut," she exclaimed in wonder. "It wasn't you it was meant for." Then she was rolling on the grass and was howling, "It's you that's cut and it should be me. I didn't mean that to happen to you. You're the last person I'd want to do harm to, Ren. I'm telling you, Ren. Truly. That cut wasn't meant for you."

"You didn't do it. It was me, dragging the knife away. I don't think it's very deep." Contradicting her, the blood continued to run; it formed a soft cone at the base of her thumb and dropped onto her boot. Ren wondered how long it would be before she had none left.

Lil was curled on the ground; her clothes were patched with damp. Her howling had subsided, but Ren suspected that Lil was waiting her chance to spring up and search for the knife.

"I can't bandage this by myself, not with one hand." Ren was pleased with this cunning. Stretching down, she said, "Come on, you'll have to help me." Lil nodded and together they returned to the trailer.

"It needs washing," Lil said mechanically.

"What with?"

"A diaper would have done, but . . ."

They were all soiled; they covered the buggy in damp, slimy hanks. "What a stink!" Lil's nostrils were twitching. "The whole place is a mess."

"I hadn't noticed."

"It's worse than that cave I found you in. It'll have to be cleaned out."

Lil did this after they had torn a shirt into strips and bandaged Ren's palm. She scrambled around, gathered up litter, washed out cans, shook the sleeping bags, while Ren fetched more wood for the fire. Lil explained, "The clothes need an airing and we can hang them near it." To do that, she made coat stands with stakes that she drove into the ground.

"I like that." Ren felt that, despite her energy, Lil still needed encouragement. She chatted: "It's nice to have a fire without risks. Hilary and Brocket saw void officials rounding people up. Brocket says they won't do it anymore till the spring. The patrolmen go off duty in the winter."

Lil showed no interest.

Ren decided that this was not the moment to tell her about Raymond. "What's the matter, Lil?"

Lil's eyes were on the fabric binding Ren's hand. There was a soggy patch in the center where the blood had seeped through. "It doesn't hurt," Ren assured her, thinking, Any minute now, she'll be out searching for that knife. She slid over to Found. "I reckon that antibiotic is working. Look!"

But Lil did not stir. "Brocket's gone after Mrs. Gimmer, hasn't he? So it'll all come out. But I had to get Found back, didn't I?"

"Yes, and you did."

"I've been drilled, you see, but I've never done it."

"Done it?"

"I wasn't taught on these uplands, where you don't know what's under your feet. They didn't think of that. They should've trained us for it, shouldn't they? I mean, is it fair? Am I to blame?"

"Nobody says you are. Cob stole Found."

"What's stealing? I've stolen. We all do."

"Not babies."

"But it's better to steal them, to steal because you intend to look after them, than to throw them out. Yet nobody who dumps them gets what Cob got. It wasn't deserved. She was ugly and old and stinking and savage as a wild beast, but she didn't deserve what she got. Nobody ever mentioned that. It was simple. If anyone puts up a fight, they used to say, he is the enemy. Don't think. Act."

"They knew best, Lil." Astonished, Ren thought, I'm saying this to a street person! I'm saying her people should live like that!

Lil looked at her. "You've been brought up to believe the grown-ups know best. We both have. They say, Listen to us and you'll learn. But there are things they don't teach. Perhaps they can't. Perhaps they don't know how."

"Lil, it's over." She no longer wanted to hear the details of the fight with Cob. "You did what you had to. Nobody taught me anything like that."

"There wasn't the need. You lived behind squads of guards."

"They weren't any help when I was brought here. What would've happened to me if you hadn't come?"

For a moment Lil smiled. "You'd have got by." Then she said, "They gave me plenty of training, Ren, but they left something out. I did what they taught me, but they didn't tell me how it would *feel*."

It was twilight and Ren was stoking up the fire when the boys returned.

Hilary's greeting was, "How is she? You managed the next injection? Is she taking fluids?" Satisfied with Ren's answer, he said, "I'll have a look, then I'm turning in. If Found continues to improve, I'm off early tomorrow."

"Where to?" Ren asked Brocket as Hilary left them.

"He's going back to Raymond, see if he can hurry up getting you and Found to Greta."

"He's going to a lot of trouble."

Brocket was silent, looking into the fire.

"But he hasn't been half so much help as you."

"He had the antibiotics."

"They wouldn't have been in time if you hadn't forced the pace and taken shortcuts. He told me. And he described that gorge. He said he would've been a goner, but you—"

Brocket interrupted. "What's that bandage for?"

"I cut myself. With Lil's knife. She found it in your pack and she was trying . . ." but she did not continue, sensing that Brocket was not listening. "I'll tell you one day."

He shook his head. "You'll be gone."

Ren felt guilty. "I couldn't live here forever, could I? I mean—how could I?—I haven't been brought up here. And you've got Annie Gimmer."

Brocket kicked at the edge of the fire, making the flames spurt. "She's dead."

Ren could not answer him. She did not know what to say.

"Dead and buried. Hilary and me buried her in the cave." He sat down and fiddled with one of the stakes that was ready for burning. "We couldn't lay her in very deep because of the rock, but there was mud and pebbles to cover her and that had to suffice. We didn't think anything would get to her, not like once. Years and years ago. They found bones there, you see. Layers of them. Elephants and lions and hippopotamuses, then wooly rhinos that came with the ice. There was always some animal or other living in that cave; people, too. Anyway, Mrs. Gimmer's there now."

"Why do you call her Mrs. Gimmer, Brocket?"

"That was her name."

"But she looked after you as if you were her son."

"Well, I couldn't call her 'Mother'; I had to keep that in case the real one turned up."

"Oh, Brocket." She put her hands over her face.

"It's not for you to cry about." He took the stake and poked it among the glowing embers. At last he said, "And Mrs. Gimmer had to go sometime. She was very old."

The tears were washing down Ren's cheeks, dripping off her chin. "It's not only her, Annie Gimmer." She was thinking of her own mother, of the new baby, of Found left on the old cattle trail, strapped into the buggy, alone.

"I wish you'd stop it, Ren. You'll start me off."

She managed, "I'm sorry. I should be glad. I mean, it's over, so I shouldn't be like this. I'll be safe with Greta . . ."

"Like you wanted, and I'm glad, too."

". . . but you'll be here, in these hills, by yourself."

"I won't. I'll be with Hilary. We've got it all arranged."

"How?"

"It was his idea. He said, as we are both . . ." Brocket paused to steady his breath. "As we're both without anyone, we might as well join up. He says I can help him. It's about that book his dad started. Only, Hilary has been thinking we could add other things. Not have it just full of the landscape things, but put in other things as well. He says I can say what Mrs. Gimmer used to tell me, and that can go in."

"I'll read it." Her tears were drying now.

"I'll have to polish up this reading job myself. I'm a bit out of practice." He added, with some of his former humor, "It's a day or two since I read a can! But I'm reminded of something." He opened his parka and reached into the lining. "I brought this from that library. It's for you."

In the firelight the cover was warm, rosy; the gilt on the leather spine glinted. Ren turned the pages carefully; they were creamy and soft. "I can't look right through till I've washed my hands."

"I took a glance, but I couldn't make it all out. I expect you can give me the gist."

"Of course I can."

"There are pictures, too."

"Yes." Her finger had found the illustration he had stopped at.

"I thought you'd like that one," he told her. "She looks like you."

"I'm not so pretty." She would have liked to say, But you're nicer than this boy is, Brocket. "It's a beautiful book, much better than audio printouts. I'll read it a lot. I'll read it to Found, too." He had given her blackberries and a witch stone and now a book. Each time it had been the best possible present. "I wish I had something for you."

"I don't mind."

There were movements behind them, then Hilary's voice. "Lil's having bad dreams. Something to do with a narrow space; and since a trailer is no cure for claustrophobia, I've brought her out."

"I wish you'd leave me alone," she objected.

"You stopped me from getting to sleep."

"I've never met anyone so bossy." However, she squatted

by the fire. "He's even brought blankets," she mocked as Hilary draped one over her and handed round the rest.

"A fire doesn't keep your back warm," he said.

"As if I don't know that! I've sat by more fires like this than you've had hot dinners."

"That wouldn't be difficult, measured by this week," he told her, and they all smiled. "I'll bring back more food when I've seen Raymond."

"He's told me." Lil addressed Ren. "So, Madge hadn't forgotten about you. And that man Raymond says there'll be a home for Found."

"He thinks Greta might have her as well as me."

"Yes. That'd be nice."

"Won't you stay with us too, Lil?"

She shook her head. "Street people aren't welcome as lodgers."

"Of course they are," Hilary protested. "Where Ren's going, people don't make such distinctions."

She smiled. "That'd take some getting used to! I don't think I want to give it a try at the moment."

Brocket asked, "So what'll you do, Lil?"

"I'm going farther north. Where my great-great-grandfather came from. I want to see what it's like. There are lakes; I'll teach myself to swim. So, first I'll find the depot where the freight stops after inspection and I'll persuade a driver to take me over the border."

"That's very risky," Hilary reminded her. "There must be safer ways. I'll ask Raymond. While you wait for something to be arranged, you can stay at my base. It's more convenient than here for making contacts."

"You don't have to bother."

Exasperated, Hilary demanded, "Why can't you accept help?"

"I was taught to look after myself."

"So what?" he snorted. "You should stop being so obstinate. You'd try the patience of a saint."

"I haven't met one, that I know of, to give it a test." Then suddenly she laughed. "But your place does sound better than this trailer, so I'll stay there till we see what this Raymond of yours can fix up."

"Fine." He blushed. "I wasn't trying to interfere, you know. Just making suggestions."

She nodded. For a time they were silent, looking into the fire. "This is like home was sometimes," she murmured.

"We ought to go inside," Brocket said. "It's growing cold."

In answer, Lil stretched for more wood and thrust it into the flames.

"You can't stay out all night, Lil."

"I'm not going in. It's too closed up."

They recalled her reference to horses chasing her people, herding them in passages from which there was no escape.

"Is that what you were dreaming about?" Ren asked her.

Lil shook her head and kept her eyes on the fire. Its light blanched her cheeks, rawed the bruise on her nose, and puckered the scabs, still soft, that laced across her throat. It was possible to imagine that only a few minutes earlier she had returned from her search, bearing Found.

"You should try telling us," Brocket suggested, gentle. "It can help to . . . sort of break the spell." He glanced at Hilary. "It can work."

"That can't put it right."

He frowned, trying to understand. "Put it right?"

Ren whispered, "Perhaps if you told us, Lil, it wouldn't be so much on your mind."

"It will always be there. If I tell it, I'll be telling it for Brocket." She looked at him and considered. "Annie Gimmer wanted to know how Cob came to be where she is, and I couldn't tell her. Now that she's dead, she'll never find out. So perhaps I owe it to Brocket."

TWENTY-THREE

She crouched by the fire. The others slid nearer. Above them clouds shut away the moon, but in their faces was the warm light of the flames. Lil stared at them unblinking.

At last she said, "I've told Ren and Brocket some of it."

"Hilary knows, too."

Ren said, "You planned to attack Cob when she was putting a new bandage on her leg."

They remembered Lil's words: "First, I'll jump at her and give a massive clout to the wound; secondly, while she's rolling in pain I'll sink a rabbit punch on her neck; and thirdly, I'll grab Found and race off."

Lil gave a short laugh, mocking herself. "Plans!

"The old hag guessed them. She dallied, talking to the baby while she peeled off a strip of cloth she had bound her with. 'You're a beauty,' she said to her, 'as fine as any

I've seen and I've met a good number. They'd be out on the drovers' ways, striding, hardy and with skin brown as a horse chestnut. Sometimes I'd join them for a while, sleep under one of the wagons, share their food. They liked my stew, the little rascals; set them up. You ought to have one of your own, Cob, their people would say, but I never had.

"'Till I found Brocket. He wasn't like those striding hardy ones, not when he was dumped. He hadn't seen much sun, but he would do, I decided. Properly cared for, he would thrive. Then Annie Gimmer turned up and put an end to it.

"'How did she put an end to it? Annie pinched him from me, that's what she did. She declared I would tire of him. What a tale! Then she never let him out of her sight till he was grown. She never gave me a chance to help her raise him.'

"All this time she was sheltering Found from the cold with her great shoulders as she unwound the cloth, zipped her up again, and replaced the waterproof covering. Found didn't give a murmur, she handled her so delicate, and I was thinking, Is this the same old hag that battered Ren, knocked her out? All her talk about children and Brocket is cunning, trying to soften me up. But I forgot that the moment she held out the cloth and said, 'You bind it,' lifting the leg. 'I don't have a free hand.'

"I moved forward. I can't believe now that I could've been such a fool, but I was. I didn't hesitate for a moment or warn myself that this could be another trick. All I thought was, She says she has no free hand, but I've got two and now I can get close enough to use them.

"So I stepped across to her. I didn't see the leg swing. It struck me below the knees. Then I was falling, knocked sideways, with that filthy strip of cloth looped around my throat.

"I don't remember much about that first fight. It's mostly a jumble of flashes—pictures—while she twisted the noose at the back of my neck. My hands were flailing about, but I couldn't aim for her body. Found was still on her lap. That was a handicap for Cob, too. She couldn't get up, use her height against me, and overpower me with blows. She had to work from the length of her arm, over Found, at full stretch. So it was good sense to strangle me till I passed out, then tie me up. It seemed like hours that I was choking, and I reckon you could die from the terror of it as much as from the lack of wind. All the time her mouth was in my face, open and jagged with tusks. They began to disappear, but before I passed out, I got my hands around the noose. I felt points rake down my cheeks; then our hands fought under my chin. There was a squeal from her as a finger snapped. I heard it crack like glass in frost.

"I don't suppose I could have been unconscious more than a few moments. It was the sound of her splashing down the stream that woke me up. That's how I saw where she had gone. My hands were numb, so it took me some time to unfasten her knots, and when I had freed my ankles they refused to hold up my legs. I went the first ten yards on my knees. I'd seen her pass between high columns of rock, and I crawled into a cavern that was totally dark. I couldn't see Cob, but I could sense that there was something ahead that had delayed her: the light from her lantern reflected on it and cast a weak glint on the wet roof. I felt my way toward it, not noticing that I was wading until I heard the thud of water. I saw that the light was below me and that I was standing on the edge of a tumbling fall."

"Did you climb down?" Brocket asked, awed.

"I half slid, half jumped."

"I guessed that was where you'd been, but I hoped I was wrong. You could've reached the end of the cave by running along the top."

"I didn't know that. Anyway, I was chasing that woman."

"Without a light." He shuddered.

"Flashes came from her lantern when I reached a bend or squeezed past a column. Brocket calls it a cave," Lil addressed the others, "but it's nothing like any cave I've heard described. It's a passage, narrow as any alleyway, with a draft that pits your skin as if you're running against hail. Except you don't run. You knock against the sides, which have shelves jutting out like blades, and you stumble and trip because the floor is never even; it's never flat; the stream that flows along it hasn't worn a smooth bed. There isn't a place wide enough to take a boot, just a fissure, and your boots bridge that, or slide into it and get wedged and you are thrown on your face, struggling to pull the boot out. The only time I knew what was ahead of me was when there was no buttress or corner between me and her light, and then the sight of her was nearly as bad as the darkness and slimy rock. In the light of the lantern, her breath spouted like smoke and she filled the whole passage, an enormous beetle, her coat fanning out like wings, her legs straddling the stream, and her boots clinging to the ledges as if fitted with suckers. A bandage would flutter loose and flick behind her. It made me think of a tail or a rope ready to whip.

"Even so, I was desperate to keep close. It wasn't only that I needed the help of her light, but I wanted to know that someone else was there—even Cob. She was wild and cunning, but I preferred her to the shouts and crashing behind me that I couldn't push out of my head. From the moment I had dropped down that waterfall and was in that passage, they had been there. Call them just memories if you like, but they're as bad as what's real. Once you've been forced into some channel—a subway, a drain—and the only way out is blocked, you're stamped with it for always. In any place like it, the sweat and the smothering in your throat and the whimpers from your mouth are just the same. And I'm telling you, the shouts and the whistles and the sirens and the hooves ramming me forward and into a funnel echoed as loudly down that cave-passage as the rattles and grunts that Cob made."

A stake in the fire crackled. They moved closer together.

Lil went on. "I seemed to have run miles before I saw a square of the night sky and came to the cave's end. Outside, I could see her against the moon, limping, and although there was a good distance between us, I could hear a noise like a thin, piping wail. I knew it didn't come from the baby; she never made a sound. It seemed the most despairing cry I'd ever heard.

"But I was wrong."

Lil bowed her head and drew the blanket over her neck. Her hands trembled.

Ren leaned close to her. "You don't have to tell us, Lil. I'll stay out here with you while you sleep."

Lil shook her head. "Cob was moving very slowly now, but I couldn't gain on her. I was drenched to the bone and freezing; I had to force my feet for every step. By that time I couldn't think. I just functioned, hoping the muscles wouldn't give up. I wasn't able to work out tactics, plans, anything of that kind. I didn't wonder what might happen next. I just dragged myself forward mechanically.

"We had crossed over curving ground and were running by the side of another stream. There were trees on the skyline, standing on the crest of a knoll. The stream led us toward the knoll and seemed to disappear at its base; but before I saw where the water went, I stumbled and sent pebbles clattering.

"She swung around and shouted, 'I thought I'd seen the last of you. Get off my heels, will you! I've given you a taste of what to expect.'

"I didn't answer. We both stopped.

"'Get away with you!' she screamed, mad with frustration. 'This baby's mine. I had her first.'

"I said, 'Not for long. You parked her. By the old cattle road.'

"She was yelling curses, but I didn't listen. I was remembering all we'd been through and how we had looked after Found.

"I heard her say, 'You'll rue your interference this night,' and I watched her place the lantern on the grass and spread out the waterproof. She laid Found on it and tucked the clothes around her. Then she backed a few steps from the baby and faced me upstream.

"'You want her. I do. She goes to the one that wins,' she announced, and came at me with her fists.

"I raised my arm as a guard and managed to ward off the punch before I was kicked off my feet and bent like a sapling over a platform of stone."

"Oh, Lil," Ren moaned.

Lil stared at her and frowned, then put a hand over her eyes. "I'm sorry, Ren. It's not your face I see.

"Hers was above me, still topped by that greasy cap and so close that it blocked out the moon. I could make out the tufts of hairs in the nostrils and the skin in ridges down the cheeks and the teeth that were broken and brown as rust. Through them, her breath whistled and sickened me with its stench. No matter how hard I pushed with my hands, I couldn't move her. I didn't have enough space to swing at her; all I could do was beat my fists on her shoulders and upper arms. She didn't flinch. I was like a mouse flattened by a cat's paw, then released for a second to wriggle before being cuffed back into place. Her fingers climbed up my chest; I could see the broken one dragging; then they fastened on my throat.

"She hissed, 'I have a mind to do you in this time, but I wouldn't rest easy. I've roved the valleys all my life and I'll not take to the manner of the pack you run with.' Her hands dropped from my throat. She grabbed one of my wrists and with a great heave pushed me halfway around, forced the arm behind me and up my back.

"I heard myself screaming, but I could hear something else. It was the voice of the man who had trained us. It told me to act as if I was finished, and then there was a chance the opponent would relax. So I let my shoulders go.

"She was saying, 'I don't want blood on my conscience when I'm tending the child. So it's a case of seeing you can't hinder,' but I was listening to my instructor's voice. It was reminding me to use my feet, and the sole of my boot found a ledge of stone; that gave me a foothold and I pushed. Her weight was still on me; the pain was still lancing through my arm, but by pushing against the ledge I managed to force my hips backward. Before she could change her position, I slid from under her, unwinding myself from her grip. As I did so, I brought up a knee and punched at her with my boot. It hit her in the belly, doubled her up, and knocked her back. Then she was in the stream, winded, thrashing around, the wounded leg stiff and clumsy; it twisted and jerked.

"I scrambled toward her, knowing that somehow I had to follow up this advantage. I could see the blood spouting out of the wound and into the water, which swirled past her, frothed behind her, then suddenly disappeared. And I saw why it disappeared. It was pouring over an edge. She was trying to get upright again, only the leg wouldn't bear her. She tottered, skidded among pebbles, crashed down. Her hands dived into the stream, the fingers scrabbled for a hold on the slippery stone, but she was already sliding. It was completely quiet. I watched her, amazed, and she stared back at me as she went with the water. It seemed a long time before there was silence again after that long, splitting shriek."

No one spoke or stirred. Each wished he could paint out the scene Lil had described.

"I didn't dare get closer to where she had fallen. All I could see was the stream folding over; then it was gone. I walked a little way from it and climbed up the knoll. From there I had a view. By then I knew what to expect, but my imagination could never have prepared me for what I saw. Brocket'll know."

"Yes." His voice hardly lifted above the put-put of the flames. "It's a vertical shaft. Mrs. Gimmer said it's three hundred feet down."

"She didn't have a chance," Hilary murmured.

"It's perhaps a good thing," Brocket said grimly. "There's no way out."

"If I hadn't kicked out at her, she wouldn't have fallen into the stream. She wouldn't have slipped. She had said she didn't intend to do me in, she was just putting me out of action. Cob spared me, but I was remembering instructions. Don't you see? If I hadn't done that, she wouldn't be dead." Her voice was shrill; it jangled their heads with echoes of that last hopeless shriek.

Eventually Brocket managed, "You couldn't know that would happen, Lil. From a kick."

Ren whispered, "She wouldn't have fallen over if I hadn't given her the wound."

After a time, calmer, Lil added, "Annie Gimmer had worked it out. She'd found the lantern. She'd seen the cap; it must have caught on a ledge or shrub as Cob went down. Knowing that Cob was dead, Annie Gimmer seemed to give up. Grieving for Cob. They'd walked the drovers' ways together. I didn't like Annie Gimmer, but she'd been good, taking care of Brocket."

"She was ready to give up," Hilary suggested. "She knew Brocket could fend for himself."

Lil muttered, "I bet she wished I'd never come. So do I."

"Well, I'm glad you did," Ren said.

"I couldn't stand it any longer on the streets. I was trying to get away, but there was the baby and I got dragged in. Then look what happened."

"It hasn't been all loss," Hilary murmured. "There have been some benefits."

As he spoke, a sound came from the trailer. At first it was no more than a rustle of breath, a sigh that sharpened into a cough to clear the throat. Ren got up. "Found's awake."

The noise was growing into a grumble; it swelled as the baby's lungs filled. "She's winding herself up for a yell," Brocket said.

"It means she's getting better." Ren discovered that her

weariness had vanished and her body was no longer stiff and cold but supple and warm. Stretching her arms, she sieved the darkness through her fingers. It was silken, feathery, soft as gauze.

Then Found's cry became a wail, hungry, demanding, amplified by the wooden panels of the trailer and thrilling their ears.

"Listen to that!" Brocket said, full of admiration. "She could get prizes for it."

"I think *we* should have the prizes," Hilary said.

"Except there aren't many going in these parts." Lil mimicked Brocket's voice.

And suddenly they were laughing although their cheeks were covered with tears, and the blankets had fallen away from their shoulders, and they were jumping, beating their feet into the grass, clapping their hands, leaping together like children careless around the sparks of a bonfire, under a guardian sky.